THE ROUND DANCE (REIGEN, LA RONDE)

TRANSLATED, ANNOTATED, & ILLUSTRATED

ARTHUR SCHNITZLER

OVID PUBLISHING GROUP

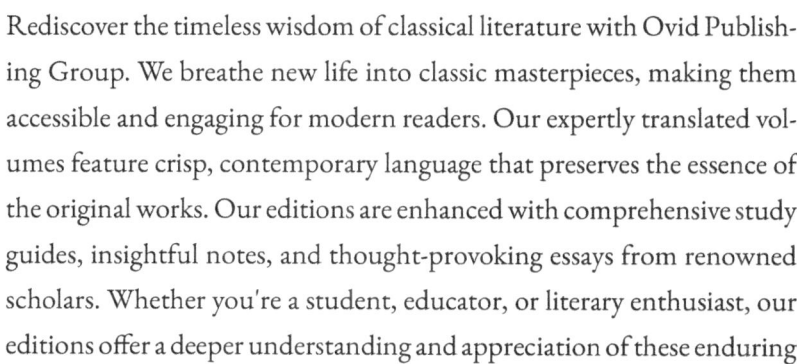

Rediscover the timeless wisdom of classical literature with Ovid Publishing Group. We breathe new life into classic masterpieces, making them accessible and engaging for modern readers. Our expertly translated volumes feature crisp, contemporary language that preserves the essence of the original works. Our editions are enhanced with comprehensive study guides, insightful notes, and thought-provoking essays from renowned scholars. Whether you're a student, educator, or literary enthusiast, our editions offer a deeper understanding and appreciation of these enduring classics. Explore the richness of ancient texts through a contemporary lens with Ovid Publishing – where timeless literature meets modern scholarship.

Click here to find more books published by Ovid Publishing Group.
https://ovidpublishing.com/

CONTENTS

INTRODUCTION TO THE ROUND DANCE

ARTHUR SCHNITZLER'S *REIGEN (THE Round Dance)*, published in 1903 and later adapted into the celebrated film *La Ronde* by Max Ophüls in 1950, stands as one of the most provocative and enduring works of modern European literature. This cycle of ten interconnected dialogues represents a masterful exploration of human sexuality, social hypocrisy, and the universal dance of desire that transcends class boundaries in fin de siècle Vienna. Within Schnitzler's extensive literary corpus, *Reigen* occupies a unique position as both his most controversial and perhaps most structurally innovative work, embodying the psychological acuity and social criticism that would define his career as one of Austria's most significant dramatists and prose writers.

Schnitzler's Literary Context and Innovation

To understand *Reigen*'s significance, one must first appreciate Schnitzler's position within the broader landscape of German-language literature at the turn of the twentieth century. Born in 1862 into a prominent Viennese Jewish family, Schnitzler trained as a physician before turning to literature, bringing to his writing a clinical understanding of human psychology that would become his trademark. His works consistently examined the psychological depths of his characters, often revealing the gap between public personas and private desires that characterised the bourgeois society of the Habsburg Empire's twilight years.

Reigen represents the culmination of Schnitzler's early experimental phase, building upon the psychological realism he had developed in earlier works such as *Anatol* (1893) and *Liebelei* (1895). However, where those plays focused on individual romantic entanglements, *Reigen* expanded its scope to encompass an entire social ecosystem, creating what literary scholar William M. Johnston has termed "a sociological X-ray of Viennese society." The work's innovative circular structure—where each dialogue shares one character with the next, ultimately returning to the prostitute who opens the cycle—creates a formal mirror for its thematic content, suggesting that human desire operates according to its own inexorable logic, indifferent to social boundaries or moral prescriptions.

The literary technique Schnitzler employs in *Reigen* reflects his deep engagement with the emerging psychological theories of his time, particularly those of Sigmund Freud, with whom he maintained a complex professional relationship. Freud himself acknowledged Schnitzler as a "colleague" who had arrived at similar insights about human nature through artistic intuition rather than scientific method. In *Reigen*, this psychological sophistication manifests in Schnitzler's ability to capture not just the external dynamics of sexual encounters, but the internal negotiations, self-deceptions, and power struggles that accompany them. Each dialogue reveals layers of meaning beneath its surface conversation, creating what critic Robert Weiss has described as "a palimpsest of desire and denial."

The Scandal and Reception

The publication and performance history of *Reigen* illustrates the work's explosive impact on contemporary society and its enduring power to provoke. Initially circulated privately among Schnitzler's literary circle, the work was not published until 1903, and even then, it appeared in a limited edition intended for mature readers. The first public performance did not occur until 1920 in Berlin, nearly two decades after its composition, and the production immediately sparked riots, legal challenges, and heated public debate that continued for years.

The scandal surrounding *Reigen* stemmed not merely from its frank treatment of sexuality—though this certainly contributed to the controversy—but from its unflinching portrayal of social hypocrisy. Schnitzler's decision to structure the work as a series of sexual encounters spanning the entire social hierarchy, from prostitute to aristocrat, challenged fundamental assumptions about class, morality, and human nature that bourgeois society preferred to leave unexamined. The work's implications were particularly threatening because it suggested that sexual desire operated as a democratising force, rendering meaningless the social distinctions upon which Habsburg society was built.

The critical reception of *Reigen* divided sharply along ideological lines. Conservative critics condemned it as pornographic and destructive to public morality, while progressive intellectuals praised its artistic courage and psychological insight. The influential critic Alfred Kerr wrote that Schnitzler had created "a work of crystalline clarity that reveals truths society would prefer to keep hidden." At the same time, his detractors accused him of cynicism and moral nihilism. This polarised response reflected broader cultural tensions in fin de siècle Europe, where traditional values increasingly clashed with emerging modernist sensibilities.

The controversy reached its peak with the 1921 Vienna production, which prompted anti-Semitic protests. Schnitzler was attacked as a Jewish pornographer, and the whole affair was called "The Reigen Scandal." Legal proceedings ultimately led to the play's ban in Austria.

The virulent opposition to *Reigen* revealed the extent to which Schnitzler's work had touched upon fundamental anxieties about sexuality, social change, and cultural identity in the post-war period. The playwright himself, deeply affected by the hostile reception, declared that he would never again permit public performances of the work. This prohibition remained in effect until after his death in 1931.

Structural Innovation and Thematic Depth

The formal structure of *Reigen* represents one of Schnitzler's most significant contributions to dramatic literature. The circular arrangement of scenes, each connected to the next through a shared character, creates a chain of human relationships that ultimately forms a closed loop. This structure serves multiple artistic functions: it reinforces the work's central metaphor of the "round dance" of desire, it demonstrates the interconnectedness of human experience across social boundaries, and it suggests the cyclical, repetitive nature of human behaviour.

Each of the ten dialogues follows a similar pattern: conversation, seduction, sexual encounter (occurring discreetly between scenes), and aftermath. However, Schnitzler's genius lies in his ability to vary this structure while maintaining its essential rhythm, creating what musicologist Carl Dahlhaus has compared to "a theme and variations in dramatic form." The prostitute and soldier who open the cycle represent the most basic, transactional form of sexual exchange, while the count and actress near the cycle's end embody the most refined and psychologically complex encounter. Yet all the dialogues share fundamental similarities, suggesting that human nature remains constant despite surface differences in education, wealth, or social position.

The thematic richness of *Reigen* extends far beyond its explicit treatment of sexuality. Schnitzler uses the sexual encounter as a lens through which to examine broader questions of power, authenticity, and social performance. Each dialogue reveals how sexual desire intersects with economic necessity, social ambition, emotional need, and psychological manipulation. The work becomes, in essence, a study of how human beings use sexuality to negotiate their relationships with others and their positions within society.

Particularly significant is Schnitzler's treatment of class dynamics throughout the cycle. While the circular structure suggests a kind of democratic equality of desire, the individual dialogues reveal how class differences profoundly shape sexual relationships. The power dynamics between the young gentleman and the parlour maid differ markedly from those between the actress and the count, yet both encounters reveal how social position influences even the most intimate human interactions. This nuanced approach prevents *Reigen* from becoming either a simple celebration of sexual liberation or a crude indictment of bourgeois hypocrisy, instead creating a complex portrait of human behaviour in all its contradictions.

Cultural Impact and Artistic Legacy

The influence of *Reigen* on subsequent literature and culture extends far beyond its immediate historical moment. The work's innovative structure has inspired numerous imitations and adaptations, while its frank treatment of sexuality helped pave the way for more open discussion of human relationships in twentieth-century literature. Writers as diverse as Tennessee Williams, Jean Anouilh, and David Hare have acknowledged Schnitzler's influence on their own explorations of sexual and social themes.

Perhaps the most significant artistic interpretation of *Reigen* came with Max Ophüls's 1950 film adaptation, *La Ronde*. Ophüls's version, while necessarily modified for cinematic presentation, captured the essential spirit of Schnitzler's original while adding layers of visual poetry and cinematic technique that enhanced the work's themes. The film's success introduced *Reigen* to a global audience and demonstrated the enduring relevance of Schnitzler's insights into human nature. Ophüls's use of a carousel as a central metaphor, his elegant camera movements that mirror the work's circular structure, and his sophisticated handling of the sexual content showed how Schnitzler's literary achievement could be successfully translated into a different artistic medium.

The film's impact was itself considerable, influencing subsequent directors such as Federico Fellini, Robert Altman, and more recently, filmmakers like Fernando Meirelles, whose 2011 adaptation updated the story to contemporary settings while maintaining its essential structure and themes. These adaptations testify to the work's continued relevance and its ability to illuminate human behaviour across different historical periods and cultural contexts.

Literary Criticism and Scholarly Assessment

Modern literary criticism has approached *Reigen* from multiple theoretical perspectives, each revealing different aspects of its complexity and significance. Feminist critics have examined how the work both reflects and challenges gender roles in fin de siècle society, noting how

Schnitzler's female characters range from victims of economic and social oppression to manipulative agents of their own desires. The prostitute Leocadia, who appears in both the first and final dialogues, has been particularly studied as a figure who embodies both the commodification of female sexuality and a certain kind of honest authenticity that contrasts with the self-deception of the bourgeois characters.

Psychoanalytic criticism has found rich material in *Reigen*'s exploration of unconscious desires and psychological defence mechanisms. Scholars have noted how each character employs different strategies to reconcile their sexual desires with their social self-image, creating layers of self-deception and rationalisation that Schnitzler exposes with clinical precision. The work's structure itself has been interpreted as reflecting the repetition compulsion that Freud would later theorise, suggesting that human beings are doomed to repeat the same patterns of desire and disappointment.

Sociological approaches to *Reigen* have emphasised its value as a historical document that illuminates the sexual and social mores of Habsburg Vienna. Historians such as Carl Schorske have argued that the work captures the particular tensions of a society in transition, where traditional aristocratic values were giving way to bourgeois respectability, which was in turn being challenged by emerging modernist sensibilities. In this reading, *Reigen* becomes not just a universal exploration of human nature, but a specific portrait of a particular historical moment and its contradictions.

Contemporary Relevance and Enduring Significance

The continued interest in *Reigen* more than a century after its composition testifies to its enduring relevance and artistic achievement. In an era when discussions of sexuality, power, and social inequality remain contentious, Schnitzler's work offers insights that feel remarkably contemporary. The #MeToo movement, debates about consent and power dynamics, and ongoing discussions about class and privilege all find precedents in the subtle psychological negotiations that Schnitzler portrayed in his ten dialogues.

The work's treatment of themes such as sexual authenticity, emotional manipulation, and the gap between public and private selves resonates particularly strongly in our current digital age, where questions of authentic self-presentation and the commodification of intimacy have taken on new dimensions. Social media's creation of new forms of performance and self-presentation would likely have fascinated Schnitzler, who understood so well how human beings construct and maintain their social identities.

Moreover, *Reigen*'s formal innovations continue to influence contemporary artists working across different media. The circular structure has been adapted for everything from hypertext fiction to interactive digital narratives, while the work's episodic format has influenced television series and web-based content that explores similar themes of interconnected relationships and social networks.

Conclusion: The Round Dance Continues

Arthur Schnitzler's *Reigen* remains one of the most psychologically astute and structurally innovative works of modern literature. Its exploration of human sexuality serves as a vehicle for broader investigations into power, authenticity, and social performance that continue to resonate with contemporary audiences. The work's controversial reception history illustrates its power to challenge fundamental assumptions about human nature and social organisation, while its artistic influence demonstrates the enduring value of Schnitzler's psychological insights and formal innovations.

In the context of Schnitzler's complete works, *Reigen* represents both a culmination of his early artistic development and a foundation for his later psychological dramas. The clinical precision with which he dissects human motivation, the subtle interplay of dialogue and subtext, and the compassionate yet unsentimental view of human weakness that characterise *Reigen* would remain hallmarks of his mature style throughout his career.

Ultimately, *Reigen* endures because it captures something essential about the human condition that transcends its specific historical moment. The "round dance" of desire that Schnitzler portrayed continues in every generation, as human beings navigate the complex relationships between their individual needs and social expectations, their authentic selves and their performed identities, their capacity for both connection and exploitation. In revealing these eternal patterns with such clarity and artistry, Schnitzler created a work that remains as relevant and provocative today as it was when it first scandalised Viennese society over a century ago.

by Arthur C. Rauscher

CHAPTER 1: THE PROSTITUTE AND THE SOLDIER

THE GAS LAMP'S AMBER glow flickered against the cobblestones as Franz made his way across the Augarten Bridge, his military boots clicking a steady rhythm. The whistle died on his lips when a voice cut through the evening air.

Prostitute

"Hello, my beautiful angel!"

He turned toward the shadow where she leaned, her dress catching what little light spilled from the street lamp. The fabric looked worn but clean, and her smile held something that wasn't quite practiced charm.

Franz kept walking.

Prostitute

"Don't you want to come with me?"

He paused, one hand adjusting the strap of his rifle.

Soldier

"Oh, I am the beautiful angel?"

Prostitute

"Sure, who else?"

She stepped closer, and he caught the scent of cheap soap and something floral.

"Do come with me. I live very near here."

Soldier

"I've no time. I must get back to the barracks."

The girl moved with him as he resumed walking, matching his pace.

Prostitute

"You'll get to your barracks in plenty of time. It's much nicer with me."

Franz slowed, studying her face in the lamplight. She couldn't be more than twenty, with dark hair pinned back and eyes that seemed older than her years.

Soldier

"That's possible."

Prostitute

"Ps-st!"

She glanced nervously down the street.

"A guard may pass any minute."

Soldier

"Rot! A guard!" Franz's hand touched the sabre at his side.

"I carry a saber too!"

Prostitute

"Ah, come with me."

He shook his head, continuing toward the bridge.

Soldier

"Leave me alone. I have no money anyway."

Prostitute

"I don't want any money."

Franz stopped dead under the next street lamp, turning to face her fully. The light revealed freckles across her nose and a small scar on her chin.

Soldier

"You don't want any money? What kind of a girl are you, then?"

Prostitute

"The civilians pay me."

She shrugged, as if this explained everything.

"Chaps like you don't have to pay me for anything."

Recognition flickered across Franz's features.

Soldier

"Maybe you're the girl my pal told me about."

Prostitute

"I don't know any pal of yours."

Soldier

"You're the one, all right! You know—in the café down the street—He went home with you from there."

The girl laughed, a sound that carried both weariness and genuine amusement.

Prostitute

"Lots have gone home with me from that café... Oh, lots!"

Franz considered this, then nodded curtly.

Soldier

"All right. Let's go!"

Prostitute

"So, you're in a hurry now?"

Soldier

"Well, what are we waiting for? Anyhow, I must be back at the barracks by ten."

They began walking together, her skirts brushing against his uniform trousers.

Prostitute

"Been in service long?"

Soldier

"What business is that of yours? Is it far?"

Prostitute

"Ten minutes' walk."

Franz stopped again, frustration creeping into his voice.

Soldier

"That's too far for me. Give me a kiss."

She rose on her toes, pressing her lips to his. The kiss lasted longer than he'd expected, and when she pulled away, her eyes had softened.

Prostitute

"I like that best anyway—when I love someone."

Soldier

"I don't. No, I can't go with you. It's too far."

Prostitute

"Say, come tomorrow afternoon."

Soldier

"Sure. Give me your address."

Prostitute

"But maybe you won't come."

Soldier

"If I promise!"

The girl bit her lower lip, then gestured toward the dark expanse beyond the bridge.

Prostitute

"Look here—if my place is too far tonight—there ... there..."

Franz followed her pointing finger toward the Danube's edge.

Soldier

"What's there?"

Prostitute

"It's nice and quiet there, too ... no one is around."

He frowned, his military bearing asserting itself.

Soldier

"Oh, that's not the real thing."

Prostitute

"It's always the real thing with me."

Her voice dropped to almost a whisper.

Prostitute

"Come, stay with me now. Who knows if we'll be alive tomorrow?"

The words struck something in Franz—perhaps the uncertainty that hung over every soldier's tomorrow.

Soldier

"Come along then—but quick."

They descended the stone steps leading down from the bridge, the girl leading the way with sure-footed confidence. The river's scent grew stronger, mixing mud and moss with the cooler air that rose from the water.

Prostitute

"Be careful! It's dark here. If you slip, you'll fall in the river."

Franz's voice carried a hollow note.

Soldier

"Would be the best thing, perhaps."

Prostitute

"Sh-h. Wait a minute. We'll come to a bench soon."

Soldier

"You seem to know this place pretty well."

Prostitute

"I'd like to have you for a sweetheart."

He almost laughed.

Soldier

"I'd fight too much."

Prostitute

"I'd cure you of that soon enough."

Soldier

"Humph—"

The girl caught his arm as his boot scraped against loose stone.

Prostitute

"Don't make so much noise. Sometimes a guard stumbles down here. Would you believe we are in the middle of Vienna?"

The city's sounds had faded to distant murmurs above them. Here, only the gentle lap of water against stone and their own breathing filled the darkness.

Soldier

"Come here. Come over here."

Prostitute

"You are crazy! If we slipped here, we'd fall into the river."

But Franz had already reached for her, his hands finding her waist.

Soldier

"Oh you—"

Prostitute

"Hold tight to me."

Soldier

"Don't be afraid..."

The soldier released his grip, stepping back from the water's edge where they'd been pressed together against the embankment wall. His uniform jacket hung askew, buttons hastily refastened in the darkness.

Prostitute

"It would've been better on the bench."

Soldier

"Here or there... Right, I'm off."

The prostitute straightened her skirts, brushing dirt from the fabric. Her hair had come loose from its pins during their encounter, dark strands falling across her face. She watched him adjust his belt, already turning away from her toward the path that led back to the bridge.

Prostitute

"Why are you rushing off like that?"

Soldier

"I've got to get to the barracks. I'm already running late."

His boots crunched on the gravel as he took several steps up the embankment. The distant sound of church bells carried across the water—half past nine. He'd have to run most of the way back to make it before the gates closed.

Prostitute

"Wait, what's your name?"

Soldier

"What's it matter to you what I'm called?"

He paused at the top of the small slope, looking down at her still standing by the water. The lamplight from the bridge cast long shadows across the riverbank, making her pale dress appear almost ghostly in the gloom.

Prostitute

"I'm called Leocadia."

Soldier

"Ha! Never heard such a name before."

The soldier shook his head, a brief laugh escaping him. Leocadia—it sounded foreign, theatrical. Like something from one of those operettas the officers' wives attended at the Burgtheater. Not the sort of name you'd expect from a woman working these streets.

Prostitute

"You!"

She called after him as he started walking away again, her voice carrying a note of desperation that made him turn back reluctantly.

Soldier

"What do you want now?"

Prostitute

"Come on, give me at least a sechserl for the caretaker!"

The words hung in the air between them. Leocadia stood with one hand extended, palm upward, though he could barely make out the gesture in the darkness. Her other hand clutched her shawl tighter around her shoulders against the evening chill rising from the Danube.

Soldier

"Ha! You think I'm your mark... Goodbye, Leocadia..."

He spat the name out with contempt, already turning his back on her. His sabre rattled against his leg as he picked up his pace, eager to put distance between himself and this encounter. The whole thing had been a mistake—he should have walked straight past her at the bridge, should have ignored her calls entirely.

Prostitute

"Scoundrel! Bastard!"

Her voice cracked as she hurled the insults after his retreating figure. The words echoed off the water, but the soldier didn't slow his stride. Within moments, his footsteps faded into the night sounds of the city—distant carriage wheels, a dog barking somewhere across the canal, the low whistle of a late barge making its way downstream.

Leocadia remained by the water's edge, watching the empty path where he'd disappeared. Her breath formed small clouds in the cold air as she stood there, one hand still unconsciously extended as if expecting coins that would never come. The church bells chimed again—three-quarters past nine now.

She pulled her shawl closer and began the slow walk back toward the bridge. Her shoes, worn thin at the heels, slipped slightly on the damp stones near the water. Each step took her further from the secluded spot where they'd been pressed together just minutes before, where his rough hands had gripped her waist and his mouth had found hers with desperate urgency.

The encounter had been brief, perfunctory. Not unusual for soldiers—they took what they wanted quickly, always mindful of curfews and duties that called them back to their regulated lives. But most at least left something, even if only a few coins. Recognition of the transaction, acknowledgment of what had passed between them.

This one had given her nothing but a false name—if Franz was even real—and disappeared into the night like smoke. Left her standing alone by the dark water with dirt on her dress and the taste of cheap tobacco on her lips.

As she reached the cobblestones near the bridge approach, Leocadia could see other figures moving in the gaslight. A carriage rattled past, heading toward the city center. Two men in top hats walked briskly in the opposite direction, their conversation a low murmur that didn't carry.

None of them looked her way.

She straightened her hair as best she could without a mirror, tucking the loose strands back behind her ears. The night was still young—plenty of time to find another customer before the taverns closed and the streets emptied. Someone who might prove more generous than the soldier with his proud uniform and empty pockets.

But first, she'd need to clean the dirt from her dress and find somewhere with better light to repair the damage to her appearance. No man wanted to pay for what looked like damaged goods, even if the damage was only superficial.

The soldier was already forgotten, just another face in the endless parade of men who passed through her nights. Tomorrow there would be others, and the day after that still more.

Chapter Notes:

1. **Augarten Bridge**: A historic bridge in Vienna spanning the Danube Canal. The Augarten district was known in the late 19th century as an area where soldiers and working-class people frequented, making it a realistic setting for this encounter.

2. **Gas lamp**: Before electric street lighting became widespread in the early 20th century, European cities used gas lamps for illumination. These produced a characteristic amber glow and required regular maintenance by lamplighters.

3. **Barracks**: Military housing where soldiers lived under strict discipline. Austrian soldiers in the late 1800s faced rigid curfews

and harsh punishments for tardiness, making Franz's concern about the time very real.

4. **Guard**: Refers to military police who patrolled the streets to maintain order and ensure soldiers returned to barracks on time. They had authority to arrest civilians and military personnel alike.

5. **Sabre**: A curved, single-edged sword that was standard equipment for Austrian cavalry and infantry officers. Carrying one was both practical and a symbol of military authority.

6. **Civilians pay me**: Prostitutes often charged different rates based on their clients' social class and perceived wealth. Soldiers, being poorly paid, were sometimes offered services for free or at reduced rates.

7. **Café**: Viennese café culture was central to social life in the late 19th century. These establishments served as meeting places across all social classes, though prostitutes working from cafés occupied a specific niche in the city's social hierarchy.

8. **Ten o'clock**: Military curfew time. Soldiers caught outside barracks after hours faced severe disciplinary action, including confinement or loss of pay.

9. **Danube**: The great river flowing through Vienna. The embankments and less-lit areas along the river were notorious meeting places for clandestine encounters.

10. **Vienna**: Capital of the Austro-Hungarian Empire at the time. Despite being a major European city, it still had many seclud-

ed areas where the contrast between urban sophistication and darker activities was stark.

11. **Sechserl for the caretaker**: A small coin (worth about 1/10 of a florin) supposedly for bribing building superintendents who might otherwise report illicit activities. Essentially she is asking for a tip. A typical daily wage during this time would have been 1 florin and an encounter with a prostitute probably half of that.

12. **Leocadia**: An unusual name for a Viennese prostitute of this era, possibly indicating foreign origins or an assumed identity. The name has Greek origins, meaning "bright" or "clear," creating irony given her circumstances.

13. **Burgtheater**: Vienna's prestigious imperial theatre, representing high culture that would be far removed from Leocadia's world. The reference emphasizes the social distance between her reality and respectable society.

CHAPTER 2: THE SOLDIER AND THE PARLOUR MAID

Sunday evening in the Prater, a large park in Vienna's Leopoldstadt district.

A path that led from the Wurstelprater, an amusement park within the larger Prater park, into the dark avenues. Here one could still hear the confused music from the Wurstelprater; also the sounds from the penny dance, an ordinary polka played by wind instruments. The soldier and the parlour maid walked together, their footsteps muffled by the soft earth beneath the trees.

Parlour Maid

"Now tell me why you absolutely had to leave so soon."

The soldier laughed awkwardly, a foolish grin spreading across his face. He'd pulled her away from the bright lights and the whirling dancers, away from the safety of the crowd where other couples spun to the cheap orchestra's tune.

Parlour Maid

"It was so lovely. I do love to dance."

The soldier's arm found her waist, his hand settling at the curve of her hip through the thin fabric of her Sunday dress. She didn't pull away, though her body tensed slightly at his touch.

Parlour Maid

"Now we're not dancing anymore. Why are you holding me so tight?"

Soldier

"What's your name? Kathi?"

Parlour Maid

"You always have some Kathi in your head."

Soldier

"I know, I know already... Marie."

The darkness pressed closer around them as they moved further from the carnival lights. Marie's white collar caught what little moonlight filtered through the heavy canopy above, making her appear almost ghostly in the gloom.

Parlour Maid

"Look, it's so dark here. I'm getting frightened."

Soldier

"When I'm with you, you don't need to be afraid. Thank God, here we are!"

His voice carried a confidence that didn't quite mask his own nervousness. This was different territory than the dockside encounters he was used to—this girl worked in a respectable household, had standards, expectations.

Parlour Maid

"But where are we going? There's no one here anymore. Come on, let's go back! And it's so dark!"

The soldier drew on his Virginia cigarette, the red end glowing bright in the darkness like a tiny beacon. The brief flare illuminated his face—young, eager, with the kind of mustache that marked him as regular army rather than a conscript.

Soldier

"It'll get lighter! Haha! Oh, you beautiful girl!"

His hands moved more boldly now, encouraged by the isolation of their surroundings. Marie's breath quickened, though whether from fear or excitement, she couldn't quite say.

Parlour Maid

"Oh, what are you doing? If I'd known this!"

Soldier

"The devil take me if any girl at Swoboda's (dance hall) was softer than you tonight, Fräulein Marie."

Parlour Maid

"Did you try with all of them like this?"

Soldier

"You notice quite a lot while dancing! Ha!"

Parlour Maid

"But you danced more with that blonde one with the ugly face than with me."

Soldier

"She's an old acquaintance of a friend of mine."

Parlour Maid

"Of the corporal with the twisted mustache?"

Soldier

"Oh no, that was the civilian, you know, the one who sat at the table with me at the beginning, the one who talks so hoarsely."

Parlour Maid

"Ah, I know. He's a cheeky fellow."

Soldier

"Did he do something to you? I'll show him! What did he do to you?"

The protective edge in his voice surprised them both. Franz felt his chest swell with an unfamiliar sense of proprietorship over this girl he'd known for barely three hours.

Parlour Maid

"Oh, nothing—I just saw how he was with the others."

Soldier

"Tell me, Fräulein Marie..."

Parlour Maid

"You'll burn me with your cigar."

Soldier

"Pardon! Fräulein Marie. But can we not be so formal? May I call you, 'Marie'?"

The suggestion hung between them, weighted with implication. To use the familiar form was to cross a boundary, to acknowledge an intimacy that went beyond their brief acquaintance.

Parlour Maid

"We're not such good friends yet."

Soldier

"Plenty of people who can't stand each other still speak informally to one another."

Parlour Maid

"Next time, when we... But, Herr Franz—"

Soldier

"You remembered my name?"

Parlour Maid

"But, Herr Franz..."

Soldier

"Just say Franz, Fräulein Marie."

Parlour Maid

"Don't be so cheeky—but quiet, what if someone came!"

Soldier

"And if someone did come, you can't see two steps ahead."

Parlour Maid

"But for God's sake, where are we going?"

Soldier

"Look, there are two just like us."

Parlour Maid

"Where? I don't see anything."

Soldier

"There... in front of us."

Through the darkness ahead, two shadowy figures moved together along the path, their whispered conversation carrying faintly on the night air.

Parlour Maid

"Why do you say: two like us?"

Soldier

"Well, I just mean, they're fond of each other too."

Parlour Maid

"But watch out... what's that... I nearly fell."

Soldier

"Ah, that's the gate to the meadow."

Parlour Maid

"Don't push me so, I'll fall over."

Soldier

"Quiet, not so loud."

Parlour Maid

"Now I really will scream. But what are you doing... but—"

Soldier

"There's not a soul far and wide now."

Parlour Maid

"Let's go back where there are people."

Soldier

"We don't need people, oh Marie, we don't need... for this... haha."

Parlour Maid

"But, Herr Franz, please, for God's sake, look, if I had... known... oh... oh... behave yourself!..."

Soldier (blissfully).

"Good God almighty... ah..."

Parlour Maid

"I can't even see your face."

Soldier

"What do you need a face for..."

The soldier struck another match, the brief flare illuminating Marie's flushed cheeks and disheveled hair before darkness swallowed them again. His hands fumbled with his uniform buttons, the brass cold against his fingers.

Soldier

"Look here, Fräulein Marie, you can't stay lying in the grass like that."

Parlour Maid

"Come on, Franz, help me up."

She reached toward him in the darkness, her voice smaller now, uncertain. The confident parlour maid who'd danced so prettily at Swoboda's seemed to have vanished, leaving behind someone younger, more fragile.

Soldier

"Right then, come along quickly."

Parlour Maid

"Oh God, Franz."

Her dress caught on something as she tried to rise—a thorn, perhaps, or just the darkness playing tricks. She tugged at the fabric, hearing a small tear that made her stomach clench with worry about what she'd tell the mistress.

Soldier

"Well now, what's wrong with Franz?"

His tone held amusement, as if her distress was somehow entertaining. He brushed grass from his trousers with careless efficiency, already looking back toward the distant lights of the dance hall.

Parlour Maid

"You're a wicked man, Franz."

Soldier

"Right, right. Come on, wait a moment."

He began to help her up, but then releases her.

Parlour Maid

"Why are you letting go of me?"

Marie looked up at him, still sitting in the damp grass, feeling suddenly cold despite the warm evening.

Soldier

"Well, I should be allowed to light my Virginia, shouldn't I?"

The cigarette glowed between his lips as he drew deeply, the red ember cast brief shadows across his face.

Parlour Maid

"It's so dark."

Soldier

"It'll be light again tomorrow morning."

Parlour Maid

"At least tell me—do you care for me?"

The question hung between them like smoke. Franz exhaled slowly, considering his words with the same care he might use cleaning his rifle.

Soldier

"Well, you must have felt that, Fräulein Marie, eh!"

He helped her stand and begins dragging her up the path.

Parlour Maid

"Where are we going then?"

Soldier

"Back, of course."

His boots crunched on fallen twigs as he stepped along the path. Marie scrambled to follow, her skirts tangling around her legs in the darkness.

Parlour Maid

"Please, don't walk so fast!"

Soldier

"What's the matter? I don't like walking in the dark."

Parlour Maid

"Tell me, Franz, do you care for me?"

Soldier

"But I just said I care for you!"

The exasperation in his voice made her wince. She'd heard that tone before—from the master of the house when she'd asked the same question twice about his breakfast preferences.

Parlour Maid

"Come on, won't you give me a little kiss?"

Soldier (excited)

"There... Listen—now you can hear the music again."

The distant strains of the polka drifted through the trees, growing stronger with each step they took back toward civilization. Franz's pace quickened noticeably.

Parlour Maid

"You don't want to go dancing again, do you?"

Soldier

"Of course, why not?"

Parlour Maid

"Look, Franz, I have to go home. They'll be scolding me already—my mistress is such a... she'd prefer if I never went out at all."

The lie came easily. Her mistress had given her the evening off without complaint, but it seemed important now to have obligations, to matter to someone.

Soldier

"Well then, go home."

Parlour Maid

"I thought, Herr Franz, that you'd walk me home."

Soldier

"Walk you home? Ha!"

Parlour Maid

"Please, it's so sad, going home alone."

Soldier

"Where do you live then?"

Parlour Maid

"It's not far at all—in Porzellangasse."

Soldier

"Really? Well, we'd be going the same way... but it's too early for me now... they're still playing, I've got extra time today... I don't need to be back at barracks until midnight. I'm going to dance some more."

Parlour Maid

"Of course, now it's that blonde with the ugly face's turn!"

Soldier

"Ha! Her face isn't ugly at all."

Parlour Maid

"Oh God, men are so wicked! You probably do this with every girl."

Soldier

"That would be too much!"

Parlour Maid

"Franz, please, not tonight—stay with me tonight—"

Soldier

"Yes, yes, all right. But I'll still be allowed to dance, won't I?"

Parlour Maid

"I won't dance with anyone else tonight!"

Soldier

"There it is already..."

Parlour Maid

"What?"

Soldier

"Swoboda's! How quickly we're back here. They're still playing the same tune... tadarada tadarada—"

He hummed along with the distant melody, his voice carrying easily through the night air. The bright windows of the dance hall beckoned ahead, promising warmth and laughter and other girls who might not make so many demands.

Soldier

"If you want to wait for me, I'll walk you home... if not... goodbye!"

Parlour Maid

"Yes, I'll wait."

They entered the dance hall together, the sudden burst of light and sound overwhelming after the quiet darkness of the park. Couples whirled past them, faces flushed with heat and exertion.

Soldier

"You know what, Fräulein Marie, why don't get yourself a glass of beer?"

He looked past her as he spoke, his eyes tracking a blonde girl at a table near by. Without warning, he approached the young blonde with an entirely different voice—cultured, proper High German that seemed to come from someone else entirely.

Soldier

"Mein Fräulein, may I have this dance?"

Chapter Notes:

1. **Prater**: A large public park in Vienna's Leopoldstadt district, originally an imperial hunting ground opened to the public in 1766. By the late 19th century, it had become a popular recreation area for all social classes.

2. **Leopoldstadt**: Vienna's 2nd district, historically home to a large Jewish population and considered somewhat bohemian. It was separated from the city center by the Danube Canal, making it feel slightly removed from respectable society.

3. **Wurstelprater**: The amusement park section within the larger Prater, featuring carnival rides, sideshows, and entertainment. "Wurstel" refers to a traditional Austrian puppet character, emphasizing the area's theatrical, slightly disreputable atmosphere.

4. **Penny dance**: Cheap public dances where couples paid a small fee (typically a few pennies) to dance to live music. These were popular among the working class and soldiers who couldn't afford more expensive entertainment venues.

5. **Polka**: A lively ballroom dance in 2/4 time that originated in Bohemia in the 1830s and became wildly popular across Europe. The polka's energetic, spinning movements made it perfect for courtship rituals.

6. **Wind instruments**: Brass and woodwind ensembles were common at outdoor dances and beer gardens because they were loud enough to be heard over crowd noise and didn't require the delicate maintenance of stringed instruments.

7. **Sunday dress**: Working-class women typically owned one good dress reserved for Sundays and special occasions. Marie wearing her best dress indicates the importance she places on this evening out.

8. **Kathi**: A common diminutive form of Katharina, one of the most popular names for working-class Austrian women in this period. Franz's assumption reveals his experience with women of Marie's social class.

9. **Marie**: Another extremely common name for Austrian

women, particularly servants. The name's popularity across social classes made it a safe guess for someone like Franz.

10. **White collar**: A starched white collar was a mark of respectability for working women, especially domestic servants who needed to maintain a clean, proper appearance for their employers.

11. **Virginia cigarette**: High-quality tobacco cigarettes, often imported or made from imported Virginia tobacco. These were more expensive than local tobacco, suggesting Franz has some disposable income or wants to impress.

12. **Regular army**: Professional soldiers who enlisted for longer terms, as opposed to conscripts doing mandatory service. Regular army men often wore distinctive mustaches as a mark of their military identity and experience.

13. **Fräulein Marie**: The formal address using "Fräulein" (Miss) with her first name represents a middle ground between complete formality (which would use her surname) and intimacy (using just her first name).

14. **Swoboda's**: A fictional dance hall, though the name is typically Czech or Slovak, reflecting the multi-ethnic nature of the Austro-Hungarian Empire and Vienna's diverse population.

15. **Corporal**: A non-commissioned officer rank above private but below sergeant. Corporals often had distinctive mustache styles as part of military grooming regulations.

16. **Civilian**: Non-military person. The distinction was important

in Austrian society, where military men held special social status but civilians often had more economic freedom.

17. **Herr Franz**: The polite formal address using "Herr" (Mr.) shows Marie maintaining social boundaries even as their interaction becomes more intimate.

18. **Informal speech (Du vs. Sie)**: German has formal (Sie) and informal (Du) forms of address. Using "Du" implied intimacy, familiarity, or social equality—a significant step in any relationship.

19. **Barracks**: Military housing where soldiers lived under strict discipline and curfews. Franz's mention of needing to return by midnight shows the constraints of military life even during leisure time.

20. **Porzellangasse**: A real street in Vienna's 9th district (Alsergrund), known for having both middle-class residences and servant quarters. The name means "Porcelain Street."

21. **Extra time**: Special permission allowing soldiers to stay out past normal curfew hours, usually granted for good behavior or special occasions. This was a valuable privilege in military life.

22. **High German**: The standardized form of German used by educated classes, as opposed to local dialects or working-class speech patterns. Franz's ability to switch linguistic registers shows his adaptability and possible social aspirations.

CHAPTER 3: THE PARLOUR MAID AND THE YOUNG GENTLEMAN

A HOT SUMMER AFTERNOON. The masters of the estate had already departed for the countryside. The cook enjoyed a day off. The parlour maid sat in the kitchen, writing a letter to the soldier, Franz, who served as her lover. A bell rang from the young gentleman's room. She stood and walked to the young gentleman's chamber.

The young gentleman lay on the divan, smoking and reading a French novel.

Parlour Maid

"Yes, young master?"

Young Gentleman

"Ah yes, Marie, ah yes, I rang, yes... what did I... yes, that's right, let down the blinds, Marie... It's cooler when the blinds are down... yes..."

Marie walked to the window and lowered the blinds. The room dimmed considerably, casting everything in a muted golden hue.

Young Gentleman (continuing to read)

"What are you doing, Marie? Ah yes. Now one can't see anything to read."

Parlour Maid

"The young master is always so industrious."

Young Gentleman (ignoring this elegantly)

"So, that's good."

Marie departed. The young gentleman attempted to continue reading, but soon let the book fall, and rang again for the maid.

Parlour Maid (appearing with a smile, she did not attempt to conceal)

Young Gentleman

"Listen, Marie... yes, what I wanted to say... is there perhaps some cognac in the house?"

Parlour Maid

"Yes, but it's locked away."

Young Gentleman

"Well, who has the keys?"

Parlour Maid

"Lini has the keys."

Young Gentleman

"Who is Lini?"

Parlour Maid

"The cook, Master Alfred."

Young Gentleman

"Well, then tell Lini."

Parlour Maid

"Yes, but Lini has the day off."

Young Gentleman

"I see..."

Parlour Maid

"Should I perhaps fetch something for the young master from the coffeehouse?"

Young Gentleman

"Ah, no... it's hot enough already. I don't need cognac. You know what, Marie, bring me a glass of water. Listen, Marie—but let it run so it's really cold."

Marie departed. The young gentleman watched her go. At the door, the parlour maid suddenly turned back toward him. The young gentleman gazed into the air.

The parlour maid turned on the water tap, letting the water run. Meanwhile, she went into her small cabinet, washed her hands, and arranged her curls before the mirror. Then she brought the young gentleman the glass of water, approaching the divan.

Young Gentleman (half sitting up as the parlour maid handed him the glass, their fingers touching)

Young Gentleman

"Thank you."

He lay back down and stretched out.

Young Gentleman

"What time is it?"

Parlour Maid

"Five o'clock, young master."

Young Gentleman

"So, five o'clock. Good."

As the parlor maid departed, she once again turned at the door. The young gentleman was watching her again. She smiled.

The young gentleman remained lying for a while, then suddenly stood up. He walked to the door, back again, lay down on the divan. He attempted to read again. After a few minutes, he rang once more.

The parlour maid appeared again with a smile she didn't attempt to hide.

Young Gentleman

"Listen, Marie, what I wanted to ask you. Wasn't Doctor Schüller here this morning?"

Parlour Maid

"No, no one was here this morning."

Young Gentleman

"That's strange. Doctor Schüller wasn't here? Do you even know Doctor Schüller?"

Parlour Maid

"Of course. That's the tall gentleman with the black full beard."

Young Gentleman

"Yes. Was he perhaps here after all?"

Parlour Maid

"No, no one was here, young master."

Young Gentleman (decisively)

"Come here, Marie."

Parlour Maid (stepping somewhat closer)

"Yes, sir."

Young Gentleman

"Closer... so... ah... I just thought..."

Parlour Maid

"What is it, young master?"

Young Gentleman

"I thought—just about your blouse... What kind is that... Well, just come closer. I won't bite you."

Parlour Maid (coming to him)

"What about my blouse? Doesn't the young master like it?"

The young gentleman took hold of her blouse, drawing the parlour maid down to him.

Young Gentleman

"Blue? That's quite a beautiful blue."

"You're very nicely dressed, Marie."

Parlour Maid

"But young master..."

Young Gentleman

"Well, what is it?"

He opened her blouse. Matter-of-factly.

"You have beautiful white skin, Marie."

Parlour Maid

"The young master flatters me."

The young gentleman kissed her breasts.

Young Gentleman

"That can't hurt."

Parlour Maid

"Oh no."

Young Gentleman

"Because you're sighing! Why are you sighing?"

Parlour Maid

"Oh, Master Alfred..."

Young Gentleman

"And what nice slippers you have..."

Parlour Maid

"But... young master... if someone rings..."

Young Gentleman

"Who would ring now?"

Parlour Maid

"But young master... look... it's so bright..."

Young Gentleman

"You don't need to be embarrassed in front of me. You don't need to be embarrassed in front of anyone... when one is so pretty. Yes, upon my soul, Marie, you are... You know, your hair even smells pleasant."

Parlour Maid

"Master Alfred..."

Young Gentleman

"Don't make such a fuss, Marie... I've seen you differently lately. When I came home the other night and got myself water, the door to your room was open... well..."

She hid her face.

Parlour Maid

"Oh God, but I had no idea that Master Alfred could be so wicked."

Young Gentleman

"I saw quite a lot then... that... and that... and that... and—"

He pointed to various spots on her body.

Parlour Maid

"But Master Alfred!"

Young Gentleman

"Come, come... here... so, yes, so..."

Parlour Maid

"But if someone rings now—"

Young Gentleman

"Now stop that already... if they do, we simply won't answer."

The bell rang.

Young Gentleman

"Damn it... And what a racket that fellow's making. Maybe he rang earlier and we didn't notice."

Parlour Maid

"Oh, I was listening the whole time."

Young Gentleman

"Well then, go look already—through the peephole."

Parlour Maid

"Master Alfred... you are... no... so wicked."

Young Gentleman

"Please, just go look now."

The parlour maid departed.

The young gentleman quickly opened the blinds.

The parlour maid appeared again.

Parlour Maid

"He's definitely gone away again. There's no one there now. Perhaps it was Doctor Schüller."

The young gentleman was unpleasantly affected.

Young Gentleman

"Very well."

The parlour maid approached him.

The young gentleman withdrew from her.

Young Gentleman

"Listen, Marie—I'm going to the coffeehouse now."

Parlour Maid (tenderly)

"Already... Master Alfred."

Young Gentleman (sternly)

"I'm going to the coffeehouse now. If Doctor Schüller should come—"

Parlour Maid

"He won't come today."

Young Gentleman (even more sternly)

"If Doctor Schüller should come, I, I... I'm at the coffeehouse."

He went into the other room.

The parlour maid took a cigar from the smoking table, slipped it into her pocket, and departed.

Chapter Notes:

1. **Estate:** Upper-class Viennese homes were often referred to as "estates" even when located in the city, reflecting the aristocratic pretensions of wealthy families who maintained both urban residences and country properties.

2. **Countryside:** During hot summer months, wealthy Viennese families would retreat to their country estates or spa towns like Baden bei Wien to escape the city's heat and unhealthy air, leaving their urban homes in the care of skeleton staff.

3. **Cook's day off:** Domestic servants typically received one afternoon or evening off per week, usually Sunday or Thursday. Senior servants like cooks had more privileges than parlour maids or scullery maids.

4. **Parlour maid:** A higher-ranking domestic servant responsible for cleaning and maintaining the family's reception rooms, serving guests, and sometimes acting as a lady's maid. This position required more refinement than a general housemaid.

5. **Divan:** A low, backless sofa or couch, often used for lounging and reading. Divans were fashionable furniture pieces in late 19th-century European homes, associated with Oriental luxury and leisurely lifestyle.

6. **French novel:** Reading French literature was a mark of ed-

ucation and sophistication among the Austrian upper classes. However, French novels also had a reputation for being risqué or morally questionable, especially among conservative circles.

7. **Blinds**: Window coverings that could be adjusted to control light and privacy. Lowering blinds during the day created an intimate, secluded atmosphere that could be seen as either practical (for heat) or suggestive.

8. **Young master**: The formal title used by servants to address the unmarried son of the household. This maintained social hierarchy while acknowledging his authority over the domestic staff.

9. **Cognac**: An expensive French brandy that was a luxury item in Austrian households. It was typically locked away both for security and to prevent servants from helping themselves to expensive spirits.

10. **Lini**: A diminutive form of names like Karolina or Magdalena, typical for Austrian domestic servants. The use of nicknames among servants created a sense of informal community within the formal household hierarchy.

11. **Master Alfred**: The combination of "Master" with his first name indicates Alfred's youth - he's old enough to command servants but young enough that using his surname alone would seem overly formal within the household.

12. **Coffeehouse**: Viennese coffeehouses were central to the city's social and intellectual life. They served not just coffee but full

meals and alcohol, and functioned as informal clubs where men could read newspapers, play cards, and conduct business.

13. **Water tap**: Running water in homes was still a relatively modern convenience in late 19th-century Vienna. The fact that Marie can let water run until it's cold indicates this is a well-appointed middle or upper-class household.

14. **Small cabinet**: Servants' quarters were typically tiny rooms, often in basements or attics. Marie having her own small space with a mirror shows she holds a relatively privileged position among the domestic staff.

15. **Five o'clock**: The afternoon hour when proper society would be taking tea or receiving visitors. The timing emphasizes the inappropriate nature of what's developing between Alfred and Marie during respectable hours.

16. **Doctor Schüller**: The surname suggests German or Austrian-Jewish origins. Doctors held high social status and would be regular visitors to wealthy households, making this a plausible excuse for Alfred's behavior.

17. **Black full beard**: Full beards were fashionable among professional men in the late 19th century and were associated with maturity, respectability, and authority - the opposite of young Alfred's character.

18. **Blue blouse**: The specific mention of color suggests this might be Marie's best blouse, perhaps new or recently cleaned. Blue was considered a modest, appropriate color for domestic ser-

vants.

19. **Beautiful white skin**: Pale skin was prized as a mark of beauty and respectability in this era, as it suggested a person didn't perform outdoor labor. For a servant, having white skin was considered particularly attractive.

20. **Slippers**: Indoor shoes worn by servants while working in the house. The fact that Alfred notices and compliments them shows his attention to intimate details of Marie's appearance.

21. **Upon my soul**: A mild oath expressing sincerity, considered more refined than stronger language. Alfred's use of such expressions shows his educated, upper-class background.

22. **The other night**: Alfred's admission that he's been watching Marie suggests this seduction has been planned, making his behavior more calculated and predatory than spontaneous.

23. **Peephole**: A small hole in doors that allowed servants to see who was calling without opening the door. This was both a security measure and a way to maintain household privacy.

24. **Cigar from the smoking table**: Taking a cigar represents Marie claiming a small trophy or compensation for what has occurred. Cigars were expensive luxury items that servants would never normally be allowed to have.

CHAPTER 4: THE YOUNG GENTLEMAN AND THE YOUNG WIFE

EVENING. A DRAWING ROOM furnished with banal elegance in a house on Schwindgasse.

The young gentleman had just entered, lighting the candles while still wearing his hat and overcoat. He opened the door to the adjoining room and glanced inside. The candlelight from the drawing room cast its glow across the parquet floor to a four-poster bed against the far wall.

A reddish gleam from the fireplace in one corner of the bedroom spread across the bed curtains.

From the dressing table, he took a spray bottle and misted the bed pillows with fine streams of violet perfume. He walked through both rooms with the spray bottle, continuously pressing the small bulb until everything smelled of violets.

He removed his overcoat and hat, settled into the blue velvet armchair in the main room, lit a cigarette, and smoked.

After a brief while, he rose again and made certain the green shutters were closed. Suddenly, he returned to the bedroom and opened the drawer of the nightstand. He felt inside and found a tortoiseshell hairpin. He searched for a place to hide it, finally slipping it into his overcoat pocket.

He opened a cabinet in the drawing room, removed a silver tray with a bottle of cognac and two liqueur glasses, and placed everything on the table.

He went back to his overcoat, from which he now took a small white package. He opened it and placed it beside the cognac, returned to the cabinet, took out two small plates and cutlery. He removed a glazed chestnut from the little package and ate it. He poured himself a glass of cognac and drank it quickly.

He checked his watch and paced about the room. Before the large wall mirror, he paused, using his pocket comb to arrange his hair and small moustache. He went to the entrance door and listened. Nothing stirred. He drew together the blue portières hanging before the bedroom door.

The bell rang. The young gentleman started slightly. He sat down in the armchair and only rose when the door opened.

A young woman entered heavily veiled to conceal her identity. She closed the door behind her, remained standing a moment, pressing her left hand to her heart as if she must master some violent agitation.

He approached her, took her left hand, and pressed a kiss upon the white, black-embroidered glove.

Young Gentleman (softly)

"I thank you."

Young Wife

"Alfred—Alfred!"

Young Gentleman

"Come, gracious lady... Come, Frau Emma..."

Young Wife

"Let me stay here a while longer—please... oh please, Alfred!"

She remained standing by the door.

The young gentleman remains, still holding her hand.

Young Wife

"Where am I?"

She looked around with curiosity.

Young Gentleman

"With me."

Young Wife

"No, I mean this house, Alfred."

Young Gentleman

"Why? It's a very distinguished house."

Young Wife

"I passed two gentlemen on the stairs."

Young Gentleman

"Acquaintances?"

Young Wife

"I don't know. It's possible."

Young Gentleman

"Pardon, gracious lady—but surely you know your acquaintances."

Young Wife

"I could not see them clearly."

Young Gentleman

"I'm not surprised. Even if they were your best friends, they couldn't have recognised you. Even I myself... if I didn't know it was you... I could not recognize you behind that veil—"

"Won't you come a little closer?... And at least remove your hat!"

Young Wife

"What are you thinking, Alfred? I told you: five minutes... No, not longer... I swear to you—"

Young Gentleman

"Then the veil—"

Young Wife

"There are two."

Young Gentleman

"Well, then, both veils—I should at least be allowed to see you."

Young Wife

"Do you love me, Alfred?"

Young Gentleman (deeply wounded)

"Emma—how can you ask me that?"

Young Wife

"It's so hot in here."

Young Gentleman

"But you're wearing your fur cape—you'll truly catch a cold."

The young woman finally entered the room and threw herself onto the armchair.

Young Wife

"I'm dead tired."

Young Gentleman

"Allow me."

He removed her veils, took the pin from her hat, and set the hat, pin, and veils aside. The young woman does not complain.

He stood before her and shook his head.

Young Wife

"What is it?"

Young Gentleman

"You've never been so beautiful."

Young Wife

"How so?"

Young Gentleman

"Alone... We're finally alone with each other—Oh, Emma—"

He sank down beside her armchair, on one knee, took both her hands, and covered them with kisses.

Young Wife

"And now... let me go again. What you demanded of me, I've done."

He put his head in her lap.

"You promised me you'd be good."

Young Gentleman

"Yes."

Young Wife

"One suffocates in this room."

Young Gentleman

"You still have your cape on."

Young Wife

"Put it with my hat."

The young gentleman removed her cape and likewise placed it on the divan.

"And now—farewell—"

Young Gentleman

"Emma—! Emma!"

Young Wife

"The five minutes are long past."

Young Gentleman

"Not even one yet!"

Young Wife

"Alfred, tell me exactly what time it is."

Young Gentleman

"It's exactly quarter past seven."

Young Wife

"I should have been at my sister's long ago."

Young Gentleman

"You can see your sister anytime..."

Young Wife

"Oh God, Alfred, why did you lead me to this."

Young Gentleman

"Because I... I adore you, Emma."

Young Wife

"How many women have you said that to already?"

Young Gentleman

"Since I saw you, no one."

Young Wife

"What a frivolous person I am! If anyone had predicted this to me... just a week ago... even yesterday..."

Young Gentleman

"And the day before yesterday you already promised me..."

Young Wife

"You tormented me so. But I didn't want to do it. God as my witness—I didn't want to... Yesterday I was firmly resolved... Do you know that yesterday evening I even wrote you a long letter?"

Young Gentleman

"I received none."

Young Wife

"I tore it up again. Oh, I should have sent you that letter instead."

Young Gentleman

"It's better this way."

Young Wife

"Oh no, it's shameful... of me. I don't understand myself. Farewell, Alfred, let me go."

He embraced her and covered her face with burning kisses.

"So... keep your word..."

Young Gentleman

"One more kiss—one more."

Young Wife

"The last one."

He kissed her; she returned the kiss; their lips remained pressed together for a long time.

Young Gentleman

"Shall I tell you something, Emma? Only now do I know what happiness is."

She sank back into an armchair.

He sits on the armrest, lightly encircling her neck with one arm.

"... or rather I only now know what happiness could be."

She sighed deeply and he kissed her again.

Young Wife

"Alfred, Alfred, what are you making of me!"

Young Gentleman

"Isn't it true—it's not at all uncomfortable here... And we're so safe here! It's a thousand times better than those rendezvous outdoors..."

Young Wife

"Oh, don't remind me of that."

Young Gentleman

"I'll always think of it with a thousand joys. For me, every minute I was allowed to spend at your side is a sweet memory."

Young Wife

"Do you still remember the Industrialists' Ball?"

Young Gentleman

"Do I remember...? I sat next to you during supper, right next to you. Your husband had champagne..."

She looked at him reproachfully.

"I only wanted to speak of the champagne. Tell me, Emma, won't you drink a glass of cognac?"

Young Wife

"A drop, but give me a glass of water first."

Young Gentleman

"Yes... Where is it—ah yes..."

He pushed back the portière and went into the bedroom.

She watched him go, and he returned with a carafe of water and two drinking glasses.

Young Wife

"Where were you?"

Young Gentleman

"In the... next room."

He poured a glass of water.

Young Wife

"Now I'm going to ask you something, Alfred—and swear to me that you'll tell me the truth."

Young Gentleman

"I swear."

Young Wife

"Has there ever been another woman in these rooms?"

Young Gentleman

"But Emma—this house has stood for twenty years!"

Young Wife

"You know what I mean, Alfred... with you! At your place!"

Young Gentleman

"With me—here—Emma! It's not nice that you can think of such things."

Young Wife

"So you have... how should I... But no, I'd rather not ask. It's better if I don't ask. I'm to blame myself. Everything takes its revenge."

Young Gentleman

"What's wrong with you? What's the matter? What takes revenge?"

Young Wife

"No, no, no, I mustn't become conscious of it... Otherwise, I'd have to sink into the earth from shame."

With the water carafe in his hand, he shook his head sadly.

Young Gentleman

"Emma, if you could sense how much you hurt me."

She poured herself a glass of cognac.

"I want to tell you something, Emma. If you're ashamed to be here—if I'm therefore indifferent to you—if you don't feel that you mean all the bliss in the world to me—then you'd better go."

Young Wife

"Yes, that's what I'll do."

He grasped her hand.

Young Gentleman

"But if you sense that I can't live without you, that a kiss on your hand means more to me than all the caresses that all the women in the entire world... Emma, I'm not like the other young men who know how to court—I'm perhaps too naive... I..."

Young Wife

"But what if you are like the other young men?"

Young Gentleman

"Then you wouldn't be here today—because you're not like the other women."

Young Wife

"How do you know that?"

He drew her to the divan and sat down close beside her.

Young Gentleman

"I've thought about you a great deal. I know you're unhappy."

She looked pleased with his words.

Young Wife

"Yes."

Young Gentleman

"Life is so empty, so worthless—and then, so short—so terribly short! There's only one happiness... to find a person by whom one is loved—"

She has took a candied pear from the table, and put it in her mouth.

Young Wife

Young Gentleman

"Give me half!"

She offered it to him with her lips.

She grasped the young gentleman's hands, which threatened to stray.

Young Wife

"What are you doing, Alfred... Is that your promise?"

He swallowed the pear, growing bolder.

Young Gentleman

"Life is so short."

Young Wife

"But that's no reason—"

Young Gentleman

"Oh yes."

Her resolve grew weaker.

Young Wife

"Alfred. You promised to be good... And it's so bright..."

Young Gentleman

"Come, come, you unique, unique one..."

He lifted her from the divan.

Young Wife

"What are you doing?"

Young Gentleman

"It's not bright at all in there."

Young Wife

"Is there another room there?"

He drew her towards to other room.

Young Gentleman

"Yes, a beautiful one... and completely dark."

Young Wife

"We should stay here."

He pulled her through the portière, into the bedroom, unfastening her bodice.

"You are so... oh God, what type of woman are you making of me!—Alfred!"

Young Gentleman

"I worship you, Emma!"

Young Wife

"So wait, wait at least... Go away... I'll call you when I'm ready."

Young Gentleman

"Let me help you—let me—help—you."

Young Wife

"You're tearing everything."

Young Gentleman

"You're not wearing a corset?"

Young Wife

"I never wear a corset. Odillon doesn't wear one either. But you can unbutton my shoes."

He unbuttoned her shoes and kissed her feet.

Once, undressed she slipped into the bed.

"Oh I'm cold."

Young Gentleman

"We'll be warm soon enough."

She laughed softly.

Young Wife

"Do you think so?"

Young Gentleman (unpleasantly affected, to himself)

"She shouldn't have said that."

He undressed in the darkness.

Young Wife (tenderly)

"Come, come, come!"

Young Gentleman (thereby in better spirits again)

"Right away—"

Young Wife

"It smells of violets here."

Young Gentleman

"That's you yourself... Yes, you yourself."

Young Wife

"Alfred... Alfred!!!!"

Young Gentleman

"Emma..."

Young Gentleman

"Apparently, I love you too much... yes... I'm beside myself."

She does not respond, but looks at him with pitty in her eyes.

"All these days I've been mad. I sensed it."

Young Wife

"Don't worry about it."

Young Gentleman

"Oh, certainly not. It's quite natural, when one..."

Young Wife

"Don't... don't... You're nervous. Just calm yourself..."

Young Gentleman

"Do you know Stendhal?"

Young Wife

"Stendhal?"

Young Gentleman

"The Psychology of Love."

Young Wife

"No, why do you ask me?"

Young Gentleman

"There's a story in it that's very significant."

Young Wife

"What kind of story is it?"

Young Gentleman

"It's about a whole company of cavalry officers."

Young Wife

"I see."

Young Gentleman

"And they tell about their love adventures. And each one reports that with the woman he loved most, you know, most passionately... that she, that he... well, in short, that it happened to each one with this woman just as it happened to me now."

Young Wife

"Yes."

Young Gentleman

"That's very characteristic."

Young Wife

"Yes."

Young Gentleman

"It's not finished yet. A single one claims... it had never happened to him in his entire life, but Stendhal adds that he was a notorious braggart."

Young Wife

"I see—"

Young Gentleman

"And yet it discourages one, that's the stupid thing, however indifferent it actually is."

Young Wife

"Of course. Besides, you know... you promised me to be good."

She laughed.

Young Gentleman

"Come now, don't laugh, that doesn't improve matters."

Young Wife

"But no, I'm not laughing at all. That about Stendhal is really interesting. I always thought that only happened with older people... or with very... you know, with people who have lived a great deal..."

Young Gentleman

"What are you thinking! That has nothing to do with it. Besides, I've completely forgotten the prettiest story from Stendhal. There's one of the cavalry officers who even tells that he spent three nights or even six... I don't remember anymore, with the woman he had desired for weeks—desirée—you understand—and during all these nights they did nothing but weep from happiness... both of them..."

Young Wife

"Both?"

Young Gentleman

"Yes. Does that surprise you? I find it so understandable—precisely when one loves."

Young Wife

"But there are certainly many who don't weep."

Young Gentleman (nervously)

"Certainly... that's also an exceptional case."

Young Wife

"Ah—I thought Stendhal said all cavalry officers weep on this occasion."

Young Gentleman

"You see, now you're making fun of it after all."

Young Wife

"But what are you thinking! Don't be childish, Alfred!"

Young Gentleman

"It simply makes one nervous... Besides, I have the feeling that you're thinking about it continuously. That embarrasses me even more."

Young Wife

"I'm absolutely not thinking about it."

Young Gentleman

"Oh yes. If only I were convinced that you love me."

Young Wife

"Do you require even more proof?"

She gestured around the room.

Young Gentleman

"You see... you're always making fun."

Young Wife

"How so? Come, give me your sweet little head."

He laid his head between her breasts.

Young Gentleman

"Ah, that feels good."

Young Wife

"Do you love me?"

Young Gentleman

"Oh, I'm so happy."

Young Wife

"But you don't need to cry as well."

He moved away from her, highly irritated.

Young Gentleman

"Again, again. I begged you so much..."

Young Wife

"When I tell you that you shouldn't cry..."

Young Gentleman

"You said: cry *as well*."

Young Wife

"You're nervous, my darling."

Young Gentleman

"I know that."

Young Wife

"But you shouldn't be. It's even dear to me, that it... that we are, so to speak, as good friends..."

Young Gentleman

"There you go again."

Young Wife

"Don't you remember then! That was one of our first conversations. We wanted to be good friends; nothing more. Oh, that was beautiful... that was at my sister's, in January at the grand ball, during the quadrille... Good God, I should have left long ago... my sister is expecting me... what will I tell her... Farewell, Alfred—"

She began to get out of bed.

Young Gentleman

"Emma! You want to leave me like this!"

Young Wife

"Yes—like this!—"

Young Gentleman

"Five more minutes..."

Young Wife

"Okay. Five more minutes. But you must promise me... not to move? ... Yes?... I want to give you one more kiss goodbye... Shh... quiet... don't move, I said, otherwise I'll get up immediately, my sweet... sweet..."

Young Gentleman

"Emma... my angel..."

The room fell into a hushed stillness, broken only by the distant sound of carriages rolling over cobblestones in the street below. Alfred's breathing grew shallow as Emma leaned closer, her hair brushing against his shoulder. The violet scent that permeated the bedroom seemed to intensify in the intimate silence.

Emma's fingers traced along his chest while she whispered soft reassurances. Her touch carried both tenderness and restraint, as if she understood the delicate balance required in this moment. Alfred remained motionless beneath her touch, his earlier agitation gradually subsiding.

The golden afternoon light that had earlier filtered through the windows had given way to the deeper amber tones of early evening.

Young Wife

"My Alfred—"

Young Gentleman

"Ah, every moment with you is heaven."

Young Wife

"But now I really must go."

Her voice carried a note of wistfulness mixed with growing concern. Alfred's hand moved to capture hers, intertwining their fingers as he studied her face in the dim light. The worry lines that had appeared around her eyes spoke of obligations waiting beyond these rooms.

Young Gentleman

"Oh, let your sister wait."

But even as he spoke the words, Alfred felt the weight of the approaching evening. The responsibilities that existed outside this sanctuary pressed against the boundaries of their stolen afternoon.

Young Wife

"I must go *home*. For my sister, it's already too late. What time is it actually?"

Emma's sister would indeed be waiting, questions would need answers, and the elaborate choreography of their separate lives would resume.

Young Gentleman

"Yes, how should I determine that?"

Young Wife

"You must simply look at your watch."

Young Gentleman

"My watch is in my waistcoat."

Young Wife

"Then fetch it."

The young gentleman stood with a mighty jerk.

Young Gentleman

"Eight."

The young wife rose quickly.

Young Wife

"Good God! Quickly, Alfred, please give me my stockings. What shall I say? They'll surely be waiting for me at home... eight o'clock..."

Young Gentleman

"When shall I see you again?"

Young Wife

"Never."

Young Gentleman

"Emma! Don't you love me anymore?"

Young Wife

"That's precisely why. Give me my shoes."

Young Gentleman

"Never again? Here are the shoes."

Young Wife

"There's a shoe-buttoner in my bag. Please, quickly..."

Young Gentleman

"Here is the buttoner."

Young Wife

"Alfred, this could cost us both our necks."

The young gentleman felt most unpleasantly affected.

Young Gentleman

"How so?"

Young Wife

"Yes, what shall I say when he asks me: Where are you coming from?"

Young Gentleman

"From your sister's."

Young Wife

"Yes, if I could lie."

Young Gentleman

"Well, you must simply do it."

Young Wife

"Everything for such a man. Oh, come here... let me kiss you once more."

She embraced him.

Young Wife

"And now—leave me alone, go into the other room. I cannot dress myself when you're watching."

The young gentleman went into the salon, where he dressed himself. He ate something from the bakery goods, drank a glass of cognac.

Young Wife

"Alfred!"

Young Gentleman

"My darling."

Young Wife

"It's better that we didn't cry."

The young gentleman smiled, not without pride.

Young Gentleman

"How can you speak so frivolously?"

Young Wife

"How will it be now—when we happen to meet again sometime in society?"

Young Gentleman

"By chance—sometime... You'll surely be at Lobheimers' tomorrow too?"

Young Wife

"Yes. You too?"

Young Gentleman

"Of course. May I ask you for a dance?"

Young Wife

"Of course, I'll be there. What do you think? I would... sink into the earth."

She stepped fully dressed into the salon, taking a chocolate pastry.

Young Gentleman

"So tomorrow at Lobheimer's, that's wonderful."

Young Wife

"No, no... I shouldn't go. I'll send my regrets."

Young Gentleman

"Then we'll meet the day after tomorrow... here?"

Young Wife

"What are you thinking?"

Young Gentleman

"At six..."

Young Wife

"There are carriages at the corner, aren't there?"

Young Gentleman

"Yes, as many as you want. So the day after tomorrow here at six. Do say yes, my beloved darling."

Young Wife

"...We'll discuss that tomorrow at the Lobheimers'."

The young gentleman shook his head and embraced her.

Young Gentleman

"My angel."

Young Wife

"Don't ruin my hair again."

Young Gentleman

"So tomorrow at Lobheimers' and the day after tomorrow in my arms."

Young Wife

"Farewell..."

The young gentleman suddenly looked worried again.

Young Gentleman

"And what will you tell—*him* today?"

Young Wife

"Don't ask... don't ask... it's too dreadful. Why do I love you so! Goodbye. If I encounter people on the stairs again, I'll have a stroke. Bah!"

The young gentleman kissed her hand once more. The young wife left.

The young gentleman remained alone. He sat down on the divan, smiled to himself, and thought, *so now I have an affair with a respectable woman.*

Chapter Notes:

1. **Schwindgasse**: A real street in Vienna's 4th district (Wieden), known for its middle-class residential buildings. The name ironically means "Swindle Street," which adds a layer of meaning to the clandestine affair taking place there.

2. **Drawing room**: The main reception room in a bourgeois home, used for entertaining guests and displaying the family's social status through furniture and décor. Also called a parlour or salon.

3. **Banal elegance**: Schnitzler's critique of bourgeois taste - furnishings that appear refined but lack genuine sophistication or originality, reflecting the pretensions of the newly wealthy middle class.

4. **Four-poster bed**: A large bed with four vertical posts support-

ing a canopy or curtains. These were expensive furniture pieces associated with wealth and were often family heirlooms passed down through generations.

5. **Violet perfume**: Violets were extremely popular in Victorian and Edwardian perfumery, considered a refined, feminine scent. The artificial misting of pillows shows Alfred's calculated preparation for seduction.

6. **Silver tray**: Silver serving pieces were marks of wealth and respectability. The formal presentation suggests Alfred is trying to create an atmosphere of refined hospitality.

7. **Cognac and liqueur glasses**: High-quality French brandy and delicate glassware represent luxury and sophistication. Cognac was particularly associated with masculine refinement and seduction.

8. **Glazed chestnut**: Marrons glacés, candied chestnuts that were an expensive French delicacy. These sweets were associated with sophisticated taste and romantic occasions.

9. **Pocket comb**: Men carried small combs for grooming throughout the day. Alfred's attention to his appearance shows his vanity and concern with making a good impression.

10. **Blue portières**: Heavy curtains hung in doorways to provide privacy and warmth. Blue was considered a calming, respectable color for home décor.

11. **Heavily veiled**: Respectable married women wore veils in public to maintain anonymity during illicit activities. Multiple

veils provided additional concealment but also suggested deep shame or fear of discovery.

12. **White, black-embroidered glove**: Expensive gloves with decorative embroidery indicated wealth and refinement. The contrast of white and black may symbolize the moral ambiguity of the situation.

13. **Frau Emma**: Using "Frau" (Mrs.) with her first name maintains formal respect while acknowledging their intimacy. This form of address was typical between lovers of different social classes.

14. **Distinguished house**: Alfred's euphemism for what is likely a house of assignation - a respectable-appearing building where rooms could be rented by the hour for romantic encounters.

15. **Fur cape**: An expensive outer garment indicating Emma's upper-class status. Fur was a significant luxury that only wealthy women could afford.

16. **Industrialists' Ball**: A social event for Vienna's wealthy business class. These formal balls were important social occasions where marriages were arranged and business connections made.

17. **Corset**: The standard undergarment for respectable women, designed to create an hourglass figure. Emma's lack of a corset suggests either modern views or her preparation for this encounter.

18. **Stendhal**: Marie-Henri Beyle (1783-1842), French writer famous for psychological novels and essays on love. His "De l'Amour" (On Love) was widely read by educated Europeans.

19. **Psychology of Love**: Stendhal's treatise "De l'Amour" analyzed the emotional and psychological aspects of romantic relationships, making it popular among intellectuals but also controversial for its frank discussion of sexuality.

20. **Desirée**: French for "desired," showing Alfred's pretentious use of foreign language to discuss intimate matters. This reflects the educated class's tendency to use French for sophisticated or delicate topics.

21. **Weep from happiness**: The romantic notion that intense emotion could be expressed through tears was popular in 19th-century literature and culture, influenced by Romantic and sentimental literary movements.

22. **Lobheimers'**: A fictional wealthy family hosting social events. Such families were central to Vienna's social calendar, and their parties were important for maintaining and advancing social connections.

23. **Quadrille**: A formal ballroom dance performed by four couples in a square formation. Learning the quadrille was essential for participation in upper-class social life.

24. **Grand ball**: Elaborate formal social events requiring expensive gowns, dancing skills, and proper etiquette. These balls were crucial for maintaining social status and making advantageous connections.

25. **Carriages at the corner**: Horse-drawn cabs available for hire, providing anonymous transportation for those engaged in

clandestine activities. Their availability near places of assignation was no coincidence.

26. **Stroke**: Emma's fear of suffering apoplexy (stroke) from shock
reflects contemporary medical beliefs about the physical effects
of extreme emotion, particularly on women thought to have
delicate constitutions.

27. **Respectable woman**: Alfred's final thought reveals his satisfaction at having seduced a married woman of good social
standing, which was considered a greater conquest than success
with prostitutes or unmarried women.

CHAPTER 5: THE YOUNG WIFE AND THE HUSBAND

A COMFORTABLE BEDROOM.

It was half past ten at night. The young wife lay in bed reading. Her husband entered the room wearing his night clothes.

She didn't not look up.

Young Wife

"Are you no longer working?"

Husband

"No. I'm too tired. And besides..."

Young Wife

"Yes?"

Husband

"I suddenly felt so lonely at my desk. I felt a longing for you."

She finally looked up.

Young Wife

"Really?"

He sat on the bed beside her.

Husband

"Don't read anymore today. You'll ruin your eyes."

She closed her book

Young Wife

"What's the matter with you?"

Husband

"Nothing, my darling. I'm in love with you! You know that!"

Young Wife

"One could almost forget it sometimes."

Husband

"One *must* even forget it sometimes."

Young Wife

"Why?"

Husband

"Because otherwise marriage would be something imperfect. It wou
ld... how shall I put it... it would lose its sanctity."

Young Wife

"Oh..."

Husband

"Believe me—it's true... If we hadn't sometimes forgotten, in the five years we've been married, that we're in love with each other—we probably wouldn't be anymore."

Young Wife

"That's too complicated for me."

Husband

"The thing is simply this: we've perhaps already had ten or twelve love affairs with each other... Doesn't it seem that way to you, too?"

Young Wife

"I haven't counted!"

Husband

"If we had savoured the first one to the end, if I had surrendered myself completely to my passion for you from the beginning, it would have gone with us like the millions of other couples. We would be finished with each other by now."

Young Wife

"Ah... so that's what you mean?"

Husband

"Believe me—Emma—in the first days of our marriage, I was afraid that's how it would turn out."

Young Wife

"Me too."

Husband

"You see? Wasn't I right? That's why it's good to live together from time to time as good friends."

Young Wife

"I see."

Husband

"And so it happens that we can always experience new honeymoons together, since I never let the honeymoon..."

Young Wife

"Extend to months."

Husband

"Exactly."

Young Wife

"And now... it seems another friendship period has ended?"

He pulled her tenderly to him.

Husband

"It would appear so."

Young Wife

"But what if... it were different with me."

Husband

"It's not different with you. You're the cleverest and most delightful creature that exists. I'm very happy that I found you."

Young Wife

"That's nice, how you can court me—from time to time."

He climbed into bed with her.

Husband

"For a man who has looked around the world a bit—come, lay your head on my shoulder—who has looked around the world, marriage actually means something much more mysterious than it does for you young girls from good families. You approach us pure and... at least to a certain degree ignorant, and therefore you actually have a much clearer view of the nature of love than we do."

She laughed.

Young Wife

"Oh!"

He looked at her earnestly.

Husband

"Certainly. Because we've become completely confused and uncertain through the manifold experiences we're forced to go through before marriage. You hear much and know too much and probably read too much as well, but you don't really have a proper concept of what we men actually experience. What's commonly called love becomes thoroughly disgusting to us; because what kind of creatures are we dependent on in the end!"

Young Wife

"Yes, what kind of creatures are they?"

He smiled and kissed her forehead.

Husband

"Be glad, my child, that you've never gained insight into these circumstances. They're mostly quite pitiable beings—let's not cast stones at them."

Young Wife

"Please—this pity—That doesn't seem quite appropriate to me."

Husband

"They deserve it. You, who were young girls from good families, who could wait quietly under your parents' protection for the honourable man who desired you in marriage—you don't know the misery that drives most of these poor creatures into the arms of sin."

Young Wife

"So they all sell themselves?"

Husband

"I wouldn't say that. I don't mean only material misery. But there's also—I'd like to say—a moral misery; a deficient understanding of what's permitted, and especially of what's noble."

Young Wife

"But why should they be pitied? They're doing quite well for themselves?"

Husband

"You have strange views, my child. You mustn't forget that such beings are destined by nature to fall deeper and deeper. There's no stopping it."

She snuggled up against him.

Young Wife

"Apparently, the falling is quite pleasant."

Her comment takes him aback.

Husband

"How can you talk like that, Emma. I think that for you respectable women, there can be nothing more disgusting than all those who are not."

Young Wife

"Of course, Karl, of course. I only said it like that in jest. Go on, tell me more. It's so nice when you talk like this. Tell me something."

Husband

"What then?"

Young Wife

"Well—about these creatures."

Husband

"What's gotten into you?"

Young Wife

"Look, I asked you before, you know, quite at the beginning, I always begged you to tell me something from your youth."

Husband

"Why does that interest you?"

Young Wife

"Aren't you my husband? And isn't it downright unjust that I actually know nothing of your past?"

Husband

"You surely don't think me so tasteless that I—Enough, Emma... that would be like a desecration."

Young Wife

"And yet you have... who knows how many other women you've held in your arms just like you're holding me now."

Husband

"Don't say 'women.' You are a woman."

Young Wife

"But you *must* answer one question for me... otherwise... otherwise... there'll be nothing with the honeymoon."

Husband

"You have a way of talking... you're a mother for God's sake... our little girl is lying in there..."

He gestured to the room next door.

She snuggled tighter against him.

Young Wife

"But I'd also like a boy."

Husband

"Emma!"

Young Wife

"Go on, don't be like that... of course I'm your wife... but I'd also like to be... your mistress a little."

Husband

"Would you like that?"

Young Wife

"So—first my question."

He looked at her with curiosity.

Husband

"Well?"

Young Wife

"Was... a married woman—among them?"

Husband

"What? How do you mean?"

Young Wife

"You know very well."

Husband

"How do you come to ask this question?"

Young Wife

"I'd like to know whether... that is—such women exist... I know that. But whether you..."

Husband

"Do you know such a woman?"

Young Wife

"Surely, I don't know that myself."

Husband

"Is there perhaps such a woman among your friends?"

Young Wife

"How can I assert that with certainty—or deny it?"

Husband

"Has one of your friends perhaps once... One talks about all sorts of things when women are among themselves—has one confessed to you?"

Young Wife

"No."

Husband

"Do you have suspicions about any of your friends that she..."

Young Wife

"Suspicions... oh... suspicions."

Husband

"It seems so."

Young Wife

"Certainly not, Karl, surely not. When I think about it—I wouldn't trust any of them to do it."

Husband

"None of them?"

Young Wife

"None of my friends."

Husband

"Promise me something, Emma."

Young Wife

"What?"

Husband

"That you will never associate with a woman about whom you have even the slightest suspicion that she... doesn't lead a completely irreproachable life."

Young Wife

"Do you think I would associate with such women?"

Husband

"I know that you won't seek out association with such women. But chance could arrange it so that you... Yes, it's even very common that precisely such women, whose reputation isn't the best, seek the company of respectable women, partly to give themselves relief, partly out of a certain... how shall I say... out of a certain homesickness for virtue."

Young Wife

"I see."

Husband

"Yes. I believe what I've said is very accurate. Homesickness for virtue. Because you can believe me that these women are all actually very unhappy."

Young Wife

"Why?"

Husband

"Why, you ask, Emma? How can you even ask me that? Just imagine what kind of existence these women lead! Full of lies, malice, meanness, and full of dangers."

Young Wife

"Yes, of course. You're quite right about that."

Husband

"Truly—they pay for that bit of happiness... that bit of..."

Young Wife

"Pleasure."

Husband

"Pleasure? How could one call it pleasure?"

Young Wife

"Well—it must be something! Otherwise, they wouldn't do it."

Husband

"It's... an intoxication."

She considered this.

Young Wife

"An intoxication."

Husband

"No, it's not even an intoxication. However, it may be—dearly paid for, that's certain!"

Young Wife

"So... you've experienced that once—haven't you?"

Husband

"Yes, Emma. It's my saddest memory."

Young Wife

"Who was it? Tell me! Do I know her?"

Husband

"What's gotten into you?"

Young Wife

"Was it long ago? Was it very long before you married me?"

Husband

"Don't ask. I beg you, don't ask."

Young Wife

"But Karl!"

Husband

"She's dead."

Young Wife

"Seriously?"

Husband

"Yes... it sounds almost ridiculous, but I have the feeling that all these women die young."

Young Wife

"Did you love her very much?"

Husband

"One doesn't love liars."

Young Wife

"So why..."

Husband

"An intoxication..."

Young Wife

"So it was that after all?"

Husband

"Don't speak of it anymore, I beg you. All that is long past. I've loved only one—that's you. One loves only where there's purity and truth."

Young Wife

"Karl!"

Husband

"Oh, how secure, how comfortable one feels in such arms. Why didn't I know you as a child? I believe then I wouldn't have looked at other women at all."

Young Wife

"Karl!"

Husband

"And you're beautiful!... beautiful!... Oh come..."

He extinguished the light.

Young Wife

"Do you know what I thought about today?"

Husband

"What, my darling?"

Young Wife

"About... about... about Venice."

Husband

"The first night..."

Young Wife

"Yes... like that..."

Husband

"What then? Tell me!"

Young Wife

"You love me so tenderly today."

Husband

"Yes, so tenderly."

Young Wife

"Ah... If you always..."

She held him in her arms.

Husband

"How?"

Young Wife

"My Karl!"

Husband

"What did you mean? If I always..."

Young Wife

"Well, yes."

Husband

"Now, what would it be, if I always...?"

Young Wife

"Then I would always know that you love me."

Husband

"Yes. But you must know it anyway. One isn't always the loving husband; one must also sometimes go out into the hostile world, must fight and strive! Never forget that, my child! Everything has its time in marriage—that's precisely what's beautiful about it. There aren't many who still remember their—Venice after five years."

Young Wife

"Of course!"

Husband

"And now... good night, my darling."

Young Wife

"Good night!"

The darkness settled around them like a familiar embrace. Emma lay still, listening to her husband's breathing as it gradually deepened into sleep. The mention of Venice had stirred something within her—memories of their honeymoon, yes, but also something else entirely. The way Alfred had looked at her today, the urgency in his touch, the whispered confessions of love that felt so different from Karl's measured affections.

She shifted slightly, careful not to disturb her husband. The silk nightgown clung to her skin, still warm from their encounter. How different it felt from the afternoon's passion—this dutiful intimacy, predictable as clockwork, satisfying in its own way but lacking the dangerous thrill that had consumed her just hours before.

Karl's philosophy about marriage echoed in her mind. Friendship periods and passionate phases. Perhaps he was right. Perhaps this was how love was meant to be—steady, reliable, comfortable. But then why did her heart race when she thought of Alfred's hands on her skin? Why did the memory of his desperate whispers make her breath catch even now?

She turned onto her side, facing away from her sleeping husband. The moonlight filtered through the curtains, casting pale shadows across the familiar furniture. Their bedroom—their sanctuary, as Karl called it. The place where they'd conceived their daughter, where they'd shared countless nights of conventional matrimonial bliss. Yet tonight it felt somehow foreign, as if she were seeing it through different eyes.

The clock on the mantelpiece chimed eleven. Emma calculated the hours since she'd left Alfred's apartment. Eight hours since she'd hurried home, her skin still flushed, her lips still swollen from his kisses. Eight hours since she'd slipped back into her role as the dutiful wife, the devoted mother, the respectable woman of Schwindgasse.

Karl stirred beside her, murmuring something in his sleep. She held her breath until he settled again. How easily he slept, unburdened by secrets or guilt. His conscience was clear—his past indiscretions safely buried with that unnamed woman who had died young, as he claimed all such women did. Did he ever think of her? Did he ever wonder what might have been if he'd chosen differently?

Emma's fingers traced the edge of the blanket. Tomorrow she would see Alfred again at the Lobheimers'. They would exchange polite greetings, perhaps dance once—all perfectly proper, completely innocent to outside observers. But she would know the weight of his gaze, the meaning behind every casual touch, the promise hidden in his formal words.

The danger of it thrilled her even as it terrified her. Karl's warnings about disreputable women echoed uncomfortably. What was she becoming? Was she already one of those creatures he pitied—those women full of lies and malice and meanness? The thought made her stomach clench with shame.

She thought of their conversation earlier, Karl's condescending tone when speaking of fallen women. If only he knew that one lay beside him now, that his pure and truthful wife harbored secrets that would shock him to his core.

When had she become someone who questioned the order of things, who weighed passion against virtue and found virtue wanting? The girl who had married Karl five years ago would never have entertained such notions. But that girl was gone, replaced by this woman who lay in the darkness plotting her next secret meeting with her lover.

Her lover. The word felt strange and wonderful and terrible all at once. She was a woman with a lover now, part of that shadowy world Karl spoke of with such disdain. Yet she didn't feel malicious or mean. She felt alive in a way she hadn't for years—perhaps ever.

Chapter Notes:

1. **Half past ten at night**: A relatively late hour for domestic activities in the 1890s, when most households retired earlier due to limited artificial lighting and gas lamps.

2. **Night clothes**: Formal nightwear consisting of nightshirts for men and nightgowns for women, often made of fine cotton or silk for the upper classes. Wearing proper nightclothes was a mark of respectability.

3. **You'll ruin your eyes**: A common Victorian concern about the health effects of reading by lamplight. Eye strain was considered a serious medical issue, particularly for women who were thought to have delicate constitutions.

4. **Sanctity**: The religious and moral reverence attached to marriage as a sacrament in Catholic Austria. Karl frames their relationship in moral rather than purely emotional terms.

5. **Ten or twelve love affairs with each other**: Karl's analytical approach reflects the period's growing interest in psychology and the scientific study of relationships, influenced by thinkers

like Sigmund Freud.

6. **Young girls from good families**: The standard description for marriageable upper-class women who were expected to be virgins and largely ignorant of sexual matters when they wed.

7. **Looked around the world a bit**: A euphemistic reference to Karl's sexual experience before marriage, which was considered normal and even healthy for men but absolutely forbidden for respectable women.

8. **What kind of creatures are we dependent on**: Karl's dehumanizing language about prostitutes reflects the era's moral double standard that allowed men to use services they morally condemned.

9. **Cast stones at them**: A biblical reference (John 8:7) to the woman caught in adultery, showing Karl's self-perceived moral authority.

10. **Material misery**: The common explanation for prostitution as economic necessity, which allowed middle-class people to maintain pity rather than moral condemnation.

11. **Destined by nature to fall deeper and deeper**: The contemporary belief in moral degradation as an inevitable process, influenced by social Darwinist ideas about character and heredity.

12. **You are a woman**: Karl's distinction between his wife and "other women" maintains the madonna-whore dichotomy central to Victorian sexual morality.

13. **Your mistress a little**: Emma's provocative suggestion reveals her growing awareness of the different types of relationships between men and women, beyond the pure wife role.

14. **Was... a married woman—among them**: Emma's crucial question shows her growing understanding of her own potential for transgression, made ironic by her recent affair.

15. **Never associate with a woman about whom you have even the slightest suspicion**: Karl's strict requirements reflect the belief that moral corruption was contagious, especially among women.

16. **Homesickness for virtue**: Karl's psychological insight that immoral women miss their lost innocence, unaware that his own wife might soon experience this same nostalgia.

17. **She's dead**: The revelation that Karl's former lover has died adds tragic weight to his moral warnings and reflects contemporary beliefs about the fatal consequences of sexual transgression.

18. **One doesn't love liars**: Karl's harsh judgment shows his need to maintain moral superiority even while admitting to participation in behavior he condemns.

19. **Venice**: Their honeymoon destination, representing the height of their romantic connection and a standard against which Emma now measures both her marriage and her affair.

20. **Schwindgasse**: Emma's mental return to the street where she met Alfred earlier that day creates dramatic irony, as she lies

beside her husband while remembering her lover's touch.

21. **Her lover**: Emma's final acceptance of this identity marks her complete transformation from innocent wife to adulteress, embracing a role that Karl would find unthinkable for his "pure and truthful" wife.

CHAPTER 6: THE HUSBAND AND THE SWEET GIRL

A PRIVATE DINING ROOM in the Riedhof restaurant glowed with comfortable, modest elegance. The gas heater burned steadily, casting warm light across the intimate space. The husband and the sweet girl occupied the cozy chamber, surrounded by the remnants of their meal—cream pastries, fruit, and cheese scattered across the white tablecloth. Hungarian white wine sparkled in their glasses, catching the gaslight.

The husband reclined in the corner of the divan, drawing leisurely on his Havana cigar. Smoke curled around his satisfied features as he watched his companion with quiet contentment.

The sweet girl perched on the chair beside him, completely absorbed in spooning cream from a pastry. She savored each bite with obvious pleasure, licking the spoon clean between tastes.

Husband

"Does it taste good?"

The sweet girl continued her methodical enjoyment of the cream, unperturbed by his question.

Sweet Girl

"Oh!"

Husband

"Would you like another one?"

Sweet Girl

"No, I've already eaten too much."

The husband noticed her empty wine glass and reached for the bottle.

Husband

"Your glass is empty."

He poured the golden liquid, watching it catch the light.

Sweet Girl

"I don't want any more wine anyway."

Husband

"Come sit with me."

Sweet Girl

"In a moment... I'm not finished yet."

The husband rose from the divan and positioned himself behind her chair. His arms encircled her as he gently turned her head toward him.

Sweet Girl

"Well, what is it?"

Husband

"I'd like a kiss."

She tilted her face up and pressed her lips to his briefly.

Sweet Girl

"You're a bold man."

Husband

"That only occurs to you now?"

Sweet Girl

"Oh no, it occurred to me earlier... already on the street. You must think something terrible of me."

Husband

"Why?"

Sweet Girl

"That I went straight into a private dining room with you like this."

Husband

"Well, you can hardly say 'straight.'"

Sweet Girl

"But you know how to ask so nicely."

Husband

"Do you think so?"

Sweet Girl

"And after all, what's wrong with it?"

Husband

"Exactly."

Sweet Girl

"Whether one takes a walk or—"

Husband

"It's much too cold for walking anyway."

Sweet Girl

"Of course it was too cold."

The husband settled back down beside her, wrapping his arm around her waist and drawing her close to his side on the divan. The warmth from the gas heater enveloped them both.

Husband

"But here it's pleasantly warm, isn't it?"

Sweet Girl

Her voice came out weakly as she leaned against him.

"Well."

Husband

"Now tell me... You'd noticed me before, hadn't you?"

Sweet Girl

"Of course. Already on Singerstrasse."

Husband

"Not today, I mean. The day before yesterday, and the day before that, when I followed you."

Sweet Girl

"Lots of men follow me."

Husband

"I can imagine that. But whether you noticed me specifically."

Sweet Girl

"You know... what happened to me recently? My cousin's husband followed me in the dark and didn't recognize me."

Husband

"Did he speak to you?"

Sweet Girl

"What do you think? Do you think everyone is as bold as you?"

Husband

"But it does happen."

Sweet Girl

"Of course it happens."

Husband

"So what do you do then?"

Sweet Girl

"Well, nothing—I just don't answer."

Husband

"Hmm... but you answered me."

Sweet Girl

"Well, are you perhaps angry about that?"

The husband pulled her closer and kissed her passionately. When they parted, he smiled against her lips.

Husband

"Your lips taste like cream."

Sweet Girl

"Oh, they're naturally sweet."

Husband

"Many people have told you that?"

Sweet Girl

"Many! What ideas you get!"

Husband

"Come on, be honest once. How many have kissed that mouth already?"

Sweet Girl

"Why are you asking me that? You wouldn't believe me anyway if I told you!"

Husband

"Why not?"

Sweet Girl

"Guess."

Husband

"Well, let's say—but you mustn't be angry?"

Sweet Girl

"Why should I be angry?"

Husband

"So I estimate... twenty."

The sweet girl pulled away from him abruptly, her eyes flashing.

Sweet Girl

"Well—why not a hundred while you're at it?"

Husband

"I was just guessing."

Sweet Girl

"Well, you guessed badly."

Husband

"All right then, ten."

Sweet Girl

Her voice carried wounded pride.

"Of course! A girl who lets herself be approached on the street and goes straight to a private dining room!"

Husband

"Don't be so childish. Whether one runs around on the street or sits in a room... We're in a restaurant here. The waiter could come in any moment—there's really nothing to it..."

Sweet Girl

"That's exactly what I thought too."

Husband

"Have you been in a private dining room before?"

Sweet Girl

"Well, if I'm going to tell the truth: yes."

Husband

"You see, I like that you're at least honest."

Sweet Girl

"But not the way you're thinking again. I was in a private dining room with a girlfriend and her fiancé, once during carnival this year."

Husband

"It wouldn't be a disaster if you'd once been—with your lover—"

Sweet Girl

"Of course it wouldn't be a disaster. But I don't have a lover."

Husband

"Come on."

Sweet Girl

"My soul's truth, I don't have one."

Husband

"But you won't try to convince me that I..."

Sweet Girl

"What?... I just don't have one—haven't for more than half a year."

Husband

"Ah, I see... But before that? Who was it?"

Sweet Girl

"Why are you so curious?"

Husband

"I'm curious because I love you."

Sweet Girl

"Is that true?"

Husband

"Of course. You must notice that. So tell me."

He pressed her firmly against him, his arms tightening around her waist.

Sweet Girl

"What should I tell you?"

Husband

"Don't make me beg so long. I want to know who it was."

She laughed, a sound like silver bells in the warm room.

Sweet Girl

"Well, a man."

Husband

"So—so—who was it?"

Sweet Girl

"He looked a little like you."

Husband

"Oh."

Sweet Girl

"If you didn't look so much like him—"

Husband

"What then?"

Sweet Girl

"Well, don't ask, when you can already see that..."

Understanding dawned in the husband's eyes.

Husband

"So that's why you let me approach you."

Sweet Girl

"Well, yes."

Husband

"Now I really don't know whether I should be happy or annoyed."

Sweet Girl

"Well, if I were in your place, I'd be happy."

Husband

"Yes, well."

Sweet Girl

"And in your speech too you remind me so much of him... and the way you look at someone..."

Husband

"What was he?"

Sweet Girl

"No, the eyes—"

Husband

"What was his name?"

Sweet Girl

"No, don't look at me like that, I beg you."

The husband enveloped her in his arms. Their kiss was long and heated, the taste of wine and cream mingling between them. When she finally shook herself free and tried to stand, her movements were unsteady.

Husband

"Why are you going away from me?"

Sweet Girl

"It's time to go home."

Husband

"Later."

Sweet Girl

"No, I really must go home now. What do you think my mother will say?"

Husband

"You live with your mother?"

Sweet Girl

"Of course, I live with my mother. What did you think?"

Husband

"I see—with your mother. Do you live alone with her?"

Sweet Girl

"Yes, of course alone! There are five of us! Two boys and two more girls."

Husband

"Don't sit so far away from me. Are you the oldest?"

Sweet Girl

"No, I'm the second. First comes Kathi; she works in a flower shop, then comes me."

Husband

"Where do you work?"

Sweet Girl

"Well, I'm at home."

Husband

"Always?"

Sweet Girl

"Someone has to be at home."

Husband

"Of course. Yes—and what do you actually tell your mother when you—come home so late?"

Sweet Girl

"It's such a rarity."

Husband

"So today, for example. Your mother asks you, doesn't she?"

Sweet Girl

"Of course, she'll ask me. I can be as careful as I want, but when I come home late, she wakes up."

Husband

"So what do you tell her?"

Sweet Girl

"Well, I'll say I was at the theater."

Husband

"And she'll believe that?"

Sweet Girl

"Well, why shouldn't she believe me? I go to the theater often. Just last Sunday, I was at the opera with my girlfriend, her fiancé, and my older brother."

Husband

"Where did you get the tickets?"

Sweet Girl

"My brother is a barber."

Husband

"Yes, barbers... ah, probably a theater barber."

Sweet Girl

"Why are you questioning me like this?"

Husband

"It just interests me. And what does the other brother do?"

Sweet Girl

"He's still in school. He wants to be a teacher. Now... imagine that!"

Husband

"And then you have a little sister?"

Sweet Girl

"Yes, she's still a brat, but you have to watch her even now. Do you have any idea how corrupted girls can get into school! What do you think? Recently, I caught her out with a boy."

Husband

"What?"

Sweet Girl

"Yes! With a boy from the school across the way, she was walking in Strozzigasse at half past seven in the evening. Such a brat!"

Husband

"And what did you do about it?"

Sweet Girl

"Well, she got a beating!"

Husband

"You're that strict?"

Sweet Girl

"Well, who else should it be? The older one is at work, mother does nothing but complain—everything always falls on me."

Husband

"My God, you're sweet!"

He kissed her and became more tender, his hands moving to caress her face and neck.

"You remind me of someone, too."

Sweet Girl

"Really—who?"

Husband

"No one specific... well, just of my youth. Go on, drink, my child!"

Sweet Girl

"Yes, how old are you anyway? I don't even know what your name is."

Husband

"Karl."

Sweet Girl

"Is it possible! Your name is Karl?"

Husband

"His name was Karl, too?"

Sweet Girl

"No, but this is a pure miracle... this is... no, the eyes... The look..."

She shook her head in amazement, studying his features intently.

Husband

"And who was he—you still haven't told me."

Sweet Girl

"He was a bad man—that's certain, otherwise he wouldn't have left me sitting there."

Husband

"Did you love him very much?"

Sweet Girl

"Of course I loved him!"

Husband

"Was he a lieutenant?"

Sweet Girl

"No, he wasn't in the military. They wouldn't take him. His father has a house in the... but why do you need to know that?"

The husband kissed her again, studying her face in the gaslight.

Husband

"You actually have gray eyes. At first, I thought they were black."

Sweet Girl

"Well, aren't they beautiful enough for you?"

He kissed her on her eyes gently, and she trembled under his touch.

Sweet Girl

"No, no—I can't stand that at all... oh please—oh God... no, let me get up... just for a moment—please."

Husband

His voice grew more tender as he held her closer.

"Oh no."

Sweet Girl

"But I'm asking you, Karl..."

Husband

"How old are you? Eighteen, right?"

Sweet Girl

"Past nineteen."

Husband

"Nineteen... and I—"

Sweet Girl

"You're thirty..."

Husband

"And some over. Let's not talk about it."

Sweet Girl

"He was thirty-two when I met him."

Husband

"How long ago was that?"

Sweet Girl

"I don't remember anymore... You know, there must have been something in that wine."

Husband

"Yes, why?"

Sweet Girl

"I'm completely... you know—everything's spinning around me."

Husband

"Then hold tight to me. Like this..."

He pressed her against him and became increasingly tender. She barely resisted his advances, her protests growing weaker.

"I'll tell you something, my treasure, we could really leave now."

Sweet Girl

"Yes... home."

Husband

"Not exactly home..."

Sweet Girl

"What do you mean?... Oh no, oh no... I'm not going anywhere, what are you thinking—"

Husband

"Just listen to me, my child, next time when we meet, you know, we'll arrange it so that..."

He sank to the floor, resting his head in her lap as the gaslight flickered around them.

"This is pleasant, oh, this is pleasant."

Sweet Girl

"What are you doing?"

She kissed his hair softly, her resistance melting away like snow in spring.

"You... there must have been something in that wine—I'm so sleepy... you know, what happens if I can't get up anymore? But, but, look, but Karl... and if someone comes in... I beg you... the waiter."

Husband

"No waiter... will ever come... in here... again tonight."

The sweet girl leaned back in the corner of the divan with closed eyes.

The husband paced up and down in the small room after lighting a cigar.

A long silence stretched between them.

The husband studied the sweet girl for a long time, speaking to himself, *Who knows what sort of person this actually is—good God... So quickly... Wasn't very careful of me... Hm...*

Sweet Girl

Without opening her eyes, she spoke softly.

"There must have been something in that wine."

Husband

"Why do you think so?"

Sweet Girl

"Otherwise..."

Husband

"Why do you keep blaming everything on the wine?"

Sweet Girl

"Where are you? Why are you so far away? Come to me."

The husband moved toward her and sat down.

Sweet Girl

"Now tell me, do you really care for me?"

Husband

"You know that..." He interrupted himself quickly. "Of course."

Sweet Girl

"You know... it's just... Go on, tell me the truth, what was in that wine?"

Husband

"Yes, do you think I am a... I am a poisoner?"

Sweet Girl

"Yes, look, I just don't understand it. I'm not like that... We've only known each other since... You, I'm not like that... on my soul and God—if you would think that of me—"

Husband

"Yes—what are you worrying yourself about? I don't think anything bad of you. I just think that you love me."

Sweet Girl

"Yes..."

Husband

"After all, when two young people are alone in a room, and have supper and drink wine... there doesn't need to be anything in the wine."

Sweet Girl

"I only said it like that."

Husband

"Yes, but why?"

Sweet Girl

With a defiant tone, she replied.

"I was just ashamed."

Husband

"That's ridiculous. There's no reason for that. Especially since I remind you of your first lover."

Sweet Girl

"Yes."

Husband

"Your *first*."

Sweet Girl

"Yes..."

Husband

"Now I'd be interested to know who the others were."

Sweet Girl

"Nobody."

Husband

"That's not true, that can't be true."

Sweet Girl

"Go on, please, don't bother me about it."

Husband

"Do you want a cigarette?"

Sweet Girl

"No, thank you kindly."

Husband

"Do you know what time it is?"

Sweet Girl

"Well?"

Husband

"Half past eleven."

Sweet Girl

"Really!"

Husband

"And your mother? She's used to it, isn't she?"

Sweet Girl

"Do you really want to send me home already?"

Husband

"No, but you yourself said earlier—"

Sweet Girl

"Go on, but you're like a different person. What have I done to you?"

Husband

"But child, what's wrong with you, what are you thinking?"

Sweet Girl

"And it was only your looks, on my soul, otherwise you would have long ago... many have already asked me to go with them to private rooms."

Husband

"Well, do you want to... come here again soon with me... or somewhere else—"

Sweet Girl

"I don't know."

Husband

"What does that mean: You don't know."

Sweet Girl

"Well, when you're asking me first?"

Husband

"So when? I just want to make clear to you above all that I don't live in Vienna. I only come here from time to time for a few days."

Sweet Girl

"Oh, you're not Viennese?"

Husband

"I am Viennese. But now I live in another city..."

Sweet Girl

"Where then?"

Husband

"Oh God, that doesn't matter."

Sweet Girl

"Well, don't be afraid, I won't come there."

Husband

"Oh God, if it amuses you, you can come there too. I live in Graz."

Sweet Girl

"Seriously?"

Husband

"Well yes, what surprises you about that?"

Sweet Girl

"You're married, aren't you?"

Husband

He looked extremely astonished.

"Yes, how do you come to that?"

Sweet Girl

"It just seemed that way to me."

Husband

"And that wouldn't bother you at all?"

Sweet Girl

"Well, I'd prefer if you were single, but..."

Husband

"Yes, just tell me, how do you come to that conclusion?"

Sweet Girl

"When a man says he doesn't live in Vienna and doesn't always have time—"

Husband

"That's not so unlikely."

Sweet Girl

"I don't believe it."

Husband

"And you wouldn't have any conscience about seducing a husband to infidelity?"

Sweet Girl

"What, your wife surely doesn't act any differently than you do."

Husband

He became very indignant.

"You, I forbid *that*. Such remarks—"

Sweet Girl

"You don't have a wife, I thought."

Husband

"Whether I have one or not—one doesn't make such remarks."

He stood up.

Sweet Girl

"Karl... are you angry? Look, I really didn't know that you were married. I was just talking. Come on, come and be good again."

After a few seconds, the husband came back to her.

Husband

"You really are strange creatures, you... women." He became tender again at her side.

Sweet Girl

"Go on... it's already so late."

Husband

"Now listen to me once. Let's talk seriously with each other for once. I want to see you again, see you again often."

Sweet Girl

"Is that true?"

Husband

"But for that it's necessary... so I must be able to rely on you. I can't keep watch over you."

Sweet Girl

"Ah, I watch out for myself."

Husband

"You are... well, one can't say inexperienced—but you are young—and—men are generally a conscienceless lot."

Sweet Girl

"Oh dear!"

Husband

"I don't mean that only in a moral sense.—Well, you surely understand me."

Sweet Girl

"Yes, tell me, what do you actually think of me?"

Husband

"So—if you want to love me—only me—then we can arrange it—even though I live in Graz. Where anyone can come in at any moment, that's really not the right thing."

The sweet girl nestled against him.

Husband

"Next time... we'll be together somewhere else, yes?"

Sweet Girl

"Yes."

Husband

"Where we'll be completely undisturbed."

Sweet Girl

"Yes."

The husband embraced her passionately.

Husband

"We'll discuss the rest on the way home." He stood up and opened the door. "Waiter... the bill!"

Chapter Notes:

1. **Riedhof restaurant**: A fictional establishment representing the type of respectable restaurant in late 19th-century Vienna that offered private dining rooms for discreet meetings between

middle-class patrons.

2. **Chambre separée (Private dining room)**: French for "separate room," referring to separate chambers in restaurants that could be rented for intimate meals, ostensibly for business meetings or family celebrations, but often used for romantic assignations while maintaining social respectability.

3. **Gas heater**: Indoor heating using gas flames, a modern convenience in upscale establishments of the 1890s that provided both warmth and atmospheric lighting.

4. **Hungarian white wine**: Wine from Hungary was popular in Vienna due to the Austro-Hungarian Empire's political union. Hungarian wines were considered refined and were commonly served in better restaurants.

5. **Havana cigar**: Premium cigars imported from Cuba, a luxury item that signified wealth and sophistication. Smoking quality cigars after dinner was a mark of gentlemanly refinement.

6. **Singerstrasse**: A major street in Vienna's first district, running through the city center near St. Stephen's Cathedral. It was a fashionable area where respectable people shopped and promenaded.

7. **Sweet girl**: The literal translation of "süßes Mädel," a Viennese type representing young working-class women who were considered charming and sexually available but not prostitutes—occupying a middle ground in the sexual hierarchy.

8. **Twenty**: His estimate of her sexual partners reflects the era's

assumption that working-class women, especially those who could be "picked up" on the street, were sexually experienced.

9. **Carnival**: The pre-Lenten celebration (Fasching in Vienna) when normal social rules were relaxed and respectable people might engage in behavior usually forbidden, making it a plausible time for a chaperoned visit to a private dining room.

10. **Flower shop**: Working in a flower shop was considered a respectable job for young women, better than factory work but not as prestigious as domestic service in a good household.

11. **I'm at home**: Being "at home" indicates she helps with domestic duties and possibly takes in piecework like sewing, common for working-class families where one daughter remained home to manage household tasks.

12. **Theater barber**: Specialized barbers who worked in theaters, maintaining the hair and beards of actors. This connection explains how the family could afford opera tickets.

13. **Opera**: Attending opera was expensive entertainment, usually beyond working-class means. Free or discounted tickets through professional connections made such cultural experiences possible.

14. **Teacher**: Teaching was one of the few respectable professions open to working-class men who could obtain education, representing upward social mobility for the family.

15. **Strozzigasse**: A real street in Vienna's 8th district (Josefstadt), a middle-class residential area. The specific location adds au-

thenticity to her story about supervising her younger sister.

16. **Graz**: Austria's second-largest city, about 120 miles south of Vienna. A married man claiming to live elsewhere was a common way to maintain distance and avoid commitment in casual relationships.

17. **There must have been something in that wine**: Her repeated insistence that the wine was drugged reflects her need to maintain some sense of innocence and victimhood, refusing to acknowledge her own agency in what happens.

18. **Next time when we meet**: The husband's assumption that this will be an ongoing affair rather than a single encounter shows his experience with such arrangements and his confidence in maintaining her interest.

19. **No waiter will come in here again tonight**: His certainty about their privacy suggests this is a practiced seduction in a familiar location, indicating both his experience and the restaurant's complicity in such arrangements.

20. **Kissed her on the eyes**: Kissing someone's closed eyelids was considered an extremely intimate and tender gesture in 19th-century European culture, more romantic and spiritual than sexual. This type of kiss suggested deep affection, reverence, or a desire to protect the person's innocence. The Count's repeated focus on Leocadia's eyes and his gentle kisses there reveal his genuine emotional confusion—he's treating a prostitute with the tenderness typically reserved for a beloved or pure woman, blurring the boundaries between commercial transac-

tion and romantic feeling that his social class normally maintained strictly separate.

CHAPTER 7: THE SWEET GIRL AND THE POET

A SMALL ROOM, FURNISHED with comfortable taste. Curtains that made the room half-dark. Red shutters. A large writing desk with papers and books scattered about. A small piano against the wall.

The sweet girl and the poet entered together. The poet locked the door behind them.

Poet

"So, my treasure."

He kissed her.

Sweet Girl

She wore her hat and mantilla.

"Ah! It's beautiful here! Only you can't see anything!"

Poet

"Your eyes must get used to the darkness. Those sweet eyes."

He kissed her on the eyelids.

Sweet Girl

"But these sweet eyes won't have enough time for that."

Poet

"Why not?"

Sweet Girl

"Because I'm only staying one minute."

Poet

"Take off your hat, yes?"

Sweet Girl

"For one minute?"

The poet took the pin from her hat and set the hat aside.

Poet

"And the mantilla—"

Sweet Girl

"What do you want? I have to leave again right away."

Poet

"But you must rest! We walked for three hours."

Sweet Girl

"We rode."

Poet

"Yes, home—but in Weidlingbach we walked around for three full hours. So just sit down and rest, my love... wherever you want. Here at the writing desk—but no, that's not comfortable. Sit on the divan. Like this."

He pressed her to sit.

"If you're very tired, you can also lie down. Like this."

He laid her on the divan.

"Put your little head on the pillow."

Sweet Girl

She laughed.

"But I'm not tired at all!"

Poet

"You only think that. There—and if you get sleepy, you can also sleep. I'll be completely quiet. Besides, I can play you a lullaby... by me..."

He went to the piano.

Sweet Girl

"By you?"

Poet

"Yes."

Sweet Girl

"I thought, Robert, you were a doctor."

Poet

"Why? I told you I'm a writer."

Sweet Girl

"But writers are all doctors."

Poet

"No, not all. I, for example, am not. But how do you come to that now?"

Sweet Girl

"Well, because you say the piece you're going to play is by you."

Poet

"Yes... perhaps it's not by me either. That doesn't matter at all. What? Generally who made it, that's always irrelevant. It only has to be beautiful—don't you think?"

Sweet Girl

"Of course... it has to be beautiful—that's the main thing!"

Poet

"Do you know how I meant that?"

Sweet Girl

"What?"

Poet

"Well, what I just said."

Sweet Girl

She spoke sleepily.

"Well, of course."

The poet stood up and came to her, stroking her hair.

Poet

"You didn't understand a word."

Sweet Girl

"Come on, I'm not so stupid."

Poet

"Of course you're that stupid. But that's exactly why I love you. Ah, it's so beautiful when you women are stupid. I mean in the way that you are."

Sweet Girl

"Go on, why are you scolding?"

Poet

"Angel, little one. Isn't it true, it's comfortable lying on the soft Persian carpet?"

Sweet Girl

"Oh yes. Go on, won't you play piano for me?"

Poet

"No, I'd rather be here next to you."

He continued to stroke her hair.

Sweet Girl

"Go on, don't you want to make some light?"

Poet

"Oh no... This twilight feels so good. We were bathed in sunbeams all day today. Now we've stepped out of the bath, so to speak, and wrap ourselves... the twilight like a bathrobe." He laughed. "Ah no—that must be said differently... Don't you think?"

Sweet Girl

"I don't know."

The poet moved slightly away from her.

Poet

"Divine, this stupidity!"

He took a notebook and wrote a few words in it.

Sweet Girl

"What are you doing?"

She turned toward him.

"What are you writing down?"

Poet

He spoke quietly.

"Sun, bath, twilight, coat... like this..."

He put the notebook in his pocket and spoke loudly.

"Nothing... Now tell me, my treasure, wouldn't you like to eat or drink something?"

Sweet Girl

"I'm not really thirsty. But I'm hungry."

Poet

"Hmm... I'd prefer if you were thirsty. I have cognac, you see, but I'd have to go get food."

Sweet Girl

"Can't you have something brought?"

Poet

"That's difficult, my maid isn't here anymore. I'll go myself... what would you like?"

Sweet Girl

"But it's really not worth it, I have to go home anyway."

Poet

"Child, there's no question of that. But I'll tell you what: when we leave, we'll go somewhere together for dinner."

Sweet Girl

"Oh no. I don't have time for that. And then, where should we go? Someone we know might see us."

Poet

"Do you have so many acquaintances?"

Sweet Girl

"Only one person needs to see us, and the trouble's already made."

Poet

"What kind of trouble is that?"

Sweet Girl

"Well, what do you think, if mother hears something..."

Poet

"We can go somewhere where nobody sees us, there are restaurants with private rooms."

Sweet Girl

She sang.

"Yes, at supper in a chambre separée!"

Poet

"Have you ever been in a chambre separée?"

Sweet Girl

"If I'm to tell the truth—yes."

Poet

"Who was the lucky one?"

Sweet Girl

"Oh, that's not how you think... I was with my girlfriend and her fiancé. They took me along."

Poet

"I see. And I'm supposed to believe that?"

Sweet Girl

"You don't have to believe me!"

The poet moved close to her.

Poet

"Have you blushed now? You can't see anything anymore! I can't make out your features anymore." With his hand he touched her cheeks. "But I recognize you even like this."

Sweet Girl

"Well, just be careful you don't confuse me with someone else."

Poet

"It's strange, I can't remember anymore what you look like."

Sweet Girl

"Thank you very much!"

Poet

He spoke seriously. "You know, that's almost uncanny, I can't picture you—In a certain sense I've already forgotten you—If I couldn't remember the sound of your voice either... what would you actually be then? Near and far at the same time... uncanny."

Sweet Girl

"Go on, what are you talking about?"

Poet

"Nothing, my angel, nothing. Where are your lips..."

He kissed her.

Sweet Girl

"Don't you want to make some light?"

Poet

"No..."

He became very tender.

"Tell me, do you love me?"

Sweet Girl

"Very much... oh very much!"

Poet

"Have you ever loved anyone as much as me?"

Sweet Girl

"I already told you no."

Poet

"But..."

He sighed.

Sweet Girl

"That was my fiancé."

Poet

"I'd prefer if you wouldn't think about him now."

Sweet Girl

"Go on... what are you doing... look..."

Poet

"We can also imagine now that we're in a castle in India."

Sweet Girl

"They're certainly not as bad there as you."

Poet

"How silly! Divine—Ah, if you had any idea what you are to me..."

Sweet Girl

"Well?"

Poet

"Don't keep pushing me away; I'm not doing anything to you—for now."

Sweet Girl

"You know, my bodice is hurting me."

Poet

"Take it off."

Sweet Girl

"Yes. But you mustn't become bad because of it."

Poet

"No."

The sweet girl rose and removed her bodice in the darkness. The poet sat on the divan meanwhile.

Poet

"Tell me, doesn't it interest you at all what my last name is?"

Sweet Girl

"Yes, what is your name?"

Poet

"I'd rather not tell you what my name is, but what I call myself."

Sweet Girl

"What's the difference?"

Poet

"Well, what I call myself as a writer."

Sweet Girl

"Ah, you don't write under your real name?"

The poet moved close to her.

"Ah... no... don't."

Poet

"What a fragrance rises up. How sweet."

He kissed her breast.

Sweet Girl

"You're tearing my shirt."

Poet

"Away... away... all of that is superfluous."

Sweet Girl

"But Robert!"

Poet

"And now come into our Indian castle."

Sweet Girl

"Tell me first if you really love me."

Poet

"But I worship you."

He kissed her passionately.

"I worship you, my treasure, my spring... my..."

Sweet Girl

"Robert... Robert..."

Poet

"That was heavenly bliss... Do you still want to know what my author's name is?"

Sweet Girl

"Yes."

Poet

"I call myself Biebitz."

Sweet Girl

"Why do you call yourself Biebitz?"

Poet

"I call myself that... well, perhaps you don't know the name?"

Sweet Girl

"No."

Poet

"You don't know the name Biebitz? Ah—divine! Really? You're only saying you don't know it, aren't you?"

Sweet Girl

"On my soul, I've never heard it!"

Poet

"Don't you ever go to the theatre?"

Sweet Girl

"Oh yes—I was there just recently with someone—you know, with my girlfriend's uncle and my girlfriend, we went to the opera to see Cavalleria."

Poet

"Hm, so you never go to the Burgtheater."

Sweet Girl

"I never get tickets given to me there."

Poet

"I'll send you a ticket next time."

Sweet Girl

"Oh yes! But don't forget! Something funny though."

Poet

"Yes... funny... you don't want to go to something sad?"

Sweet Girl

"Not really."

Poet

"Even if it's a play by me?"

Sweet Girl

"Come on—a play by you? You write for the theatre?"

Poet

"Allow me, I want to make some light. I haven't seen you yet since you became my lover.—Angel!"

He lit a candle.

Sweet Girl

"Come on, I'm ashamed. Give me at least a blanket."

Poet

"Later!"

He came to her with the light, gazing at her for a long time.

Sweet Girl

She covered her face with her hands.

"Come on, Robert!"

Poet

"You are beautiful, you are beauty itself, you are perhaps even nature, you are sacred simplicity."

Sweet Girl

"Oh no, you're dripping wax on me! Look, why don't you pay attention!"

The poet set the candle away.

Poet

"You are what I have been seeking for so long. You love only me, you would love me even if I were a notions clerk. That feels good. I want to confess to you that I couldn't shake a certain suspicion until this moment. Tell me honestly, didn't you suspect that I am Biebitz?"

Sweet Girl

"But come on, I don't know what you want from me. I don't know any Biebitz."

Poet

"What is fame! No, forget what I said, forget even the name I told you. I am Robert and want to remain Robert for you. I was only joking."

He spoke lightly.

"I'm not a writer at all, I'm a clerk and in the evenings I play piano for folk singers."

Sweet Girl

"Yes, now I don't understand anything anymore... no, and how you look at someone. Yes, what is it, yes what's wrong with you?"

Poet

"It's very strange—what has almost never happened to me, my treasure, I'm close to tears. You move me deeply. We want to stay together, yes? We will love each other very much."

Sweet Girl

"You, is that true about the folk singers?"

Poet

"Yes, but don't ask further. If you love me, don't ask anything at all. Tell me, can you make yourself completely free for a few weeks?"

Sweet Girl

"How do you mean completely free?"

Poet

"Well, away from home?"

Sweet Girl

"But! How can I do that! What would mother say? And then, without me everything would go wrong at home."

Poet

"I had imagined it beautifully, living together with you, alone with you, somewhere in solitude outside, in the forest, in nature for a few weeks. Nature... in nature. And then, one day farewell—to part from each other without knowing where."

Sweet Girl

"Now you're already talking about saying goodbye! And I thought you were so fond of me."

Poet

"That's exactly why—"

He bent down to her and kissed her on the forehead.

"You sweet creature!"

Sweet Girl

"Come on, hold me tight, I'm so cold."

Poet

"It will be time for you to get dressed. Wait, I'll light a few more candles for you."

The sweet girl rose.

Sweet Girl

"Don't look."

Poet

"No."

He moved to the window.

"Tell me, my child, are you happy?"

Sweet Girl

"How do you mean that?"

Poet

"I mean in general, whether you are happy?"

Sweet Girl

"It could be better."

Poet

"You misunderstand me. You've already told me enough about your domestic circumstances. I know you're no princess. I mean, if you disregard all of that, when you simply feel yourself living. Do you even feel yourself living?"

Sweet Girl

"Do you have a comb?"

The poet went to the dressing table, gave her the comb, and watched the sweet girl.

Poet

"Good God, you look so enchanting!"

Sweet Girl

"Well... don't!"

Poet

"Come on, stay here, stay here, I'll get something for supper and..."

Sweet Girl

"But it's already much too late."

Poet

"It's not even nine yet."

Sweet Girl

"Well, be so good, then I really must hurry."

Poet

"When will we see each other again?"

Sweet Girl

"Well, when do you want to see me again?"

Poet

"Tomorrow."

Sweet Girl

"What day is tomorrow?"

Poet

"Saturday."

Sweet Girl

"Oh, I can't then, I have to go to the guardian with my little sister."

Poet

"So Sunday... hm... Sunday... on Sunday... now I'll explain something to you.—I'm not Biebitz, but Biebitz is my friend. I'll introduce you to him sometime. But Sunday there's a play by Biebitz; I'll send you a ticket and then pick you up from the theatre. You'll tell me how you liked the play, yes?"

Sweet Girl

"Now, this story with Biebitz—I'm getting quite confused."

Poet

"I'll only know you completely when I know what you felt during this play."

Sweet Girl

"I'm ready."

Poet

"Come, my treasure!"

They left together.

Chapter Notes:

1. **Small room, furnished with comfortable taste**: A typical middle-class Viennese apartment of the 1890s, representing the modest but refined living quarters of an educated professional like a poet or writer.

2. **Red shutters**: Interior shutters that could be closed for privacy and to control light. Closing them during the day created an intimate, secluded atmosphere.

3. **Writing desk with papers and books scattered about**: The romantic image of the artistic workspace, suggesting creative chaos and intellectual activity that would impress a young working-class woman.

4. **Small piano against the wall**: An upright piano was a standard furnishing in middle-class homes, indicating cultural refinement and providing entertainment before the age of recorded music.

5. **Hat and mantilla**: A mantilla is a lightweight lace or silk veil worn over the head and shoulders, popular among European women in the late 19th century for both fashion and modesty.

6. **Pin from her hat**: Women's hats were secured with long decorative pins. The poet's casual removal of her hat suggests increasing intimacy and his experience with women.

7. **Weidlingbach**: A real village on the outskirts of Vienna, popular for day trips and walks in nature. It was accessible by train and represented an escape from urban life to romantic natural

settings.

8. **Divan**: A low, backless sofa often used for lounging and reading. Divans were fashionable furniture pieces associated with Oriental luxury and bohemian artistic lifestyles.

9. **Lullaby... by me**: The poet's claim to have composed music reveals his artistic pretensions and his attempt to impress the sweet girl with his creative abilities.

10. **Robert, you were a doctor**: Her confusion about his profession reflects the common assumption that all educated men were doctors, as medicine was one of the most prestigious and recognizable professional paths.

11. **Writers are all doctors**: A misunderstanding common among working-class people who associated education and literacy primarily with the medical profession, the most visible learned profession in daily life.

12. **Persian carpet**: An expensive luxury item indicating wealth and refined taste. Persian rugs were highly prized in European homes as symbols of exotic sophistication.

13. **Twilight like a bathrobe**: The poet's metaphorical language demonstrates his literary sensibility and his habit of transforming everyday experiences into artistic observations.

14. **Notebook**: Writers commonly carried small notebooks to jot down observations, dialogue, or poetic phrases. The poet's immediate recording of his metaphor shows his opportunistic approach to inspiration.

15. **Cognac**: An expensive French brandy that was a luxury item in Austrian households, typically reserved for special occasions or to impress guests.

16. **Maid isn't here anymore**: Domestic servants typically lived in their employers' homes. The absence of his maid creates privacy but also suggests the poet may not be as wealthy as he appears.

17. **Chambre separée**: French for "separate room," referring to private dining rooms in restaurants used for intimate meals. The sweet girl's knowledge of this term suggests more worldly experience than she initially appears to have.

18. **If mother hears something**: Young unmarried women lived under strict parental supervision. Being seen in public with a man, especially in compromising circumstances, could damage both her reputation and marriage prospects.

19. **Castle in India**: An exotic fantasy setting popular in romantic literature of the era, representing escape from ordinary life into a world of sensual pleasure and adventure.

20. **Bodice**: The fitted upper portion of a woman's dress or the structured undergarment worn beneath it. Removing one's bodice was a significant step toward undressing and intimacy.

21. **What I call myself as a writer**: Many authors used pen names (nom de plume) either for artistic reasons or to separate their literary identity from their personal or professional life.

22. **Biebitz**: The poet's fictional pen name, which sounds German or Austrian. His pride in this literary identity contrasts with the

sweet girl's complete ignorance of his supposed fame.

23. **Burgtheater**: Vienna's prestigious imperial theater, founded in 1741 and considered one of the most important German-language theaters in the world. Having a play performed there represented the pinnacle of literary success.

24. **Cavalleria**: Short for "Cavalleria Rusticana," a popular one-act opera by Pietro Mascagni that premiered in 1890. It was frequently performed and accessible to middle-class audiences.

25. **Folk singers**: Street musicians and performers in taverns who entertained working-class audiences. The poet's false claim to accompany folk singers is meant to seem more humble and relatable.

26. **Sacred simplicity**: The poet's romanticization of the sweet girl's supposed innocence reflects the era's idealization of "natural" women uncontaminated by education or sophistication.

27. **Notions clerk**: A shopkeeper selling small household items like buttons, thread, and sewing supplies. This represents a modest, respectable but unglamorous middle-class profession.

28. **Guardian**: A legal guardian appointed to oversee orphaned or semi-orphaned children. The sweet girl's obligation to accompany her sister to see their guardian indicates their family's reduced circumstances.

CHAPTER 8: THE POET AND THE ACTRESS

A ROOM IN A country inn lay bathed in moonlight that spilled across the meadows and hills beyond. The spring evening air drifted through open windows, carrying with it a profound silence that seemed to hold the world in suspension.

The Poet and the Actress entered together. As they stepped inside, the light the Poet carried in his hand suddenly extinguished.

Poet

"Oh..."

Actress

"What happened?"

Poet

"The light. But we don't need any. Look, it's quite bright in here. Wonderful!"

The Actress suddenly sank down by the window, her hands folded in prayer.

Poet

"What are you doing?"

The Actress remained silent.

Poet

He moved toward her.

"What are you doing?"

Actress

She turned on him with indignation.

"Can't you see that I'm praying?"

Poet

"Do you believe in God?"

Actress

"Of course I do. I'm no pale scoundrel."

Poet

"Ah, I see."

Actress

"Come here to me, kneel down beside me. You could really pray for once too. It won't make a pearl fall from your crown."

The Poet knelt beside her and embraced her.

Actress

"Libertine!"

She rose to her feet.

"And do you know to whom I was praying?"

Poet

"To God, I assume."

Actress

Great mockery filled her voice.

"Indeed! I was praying to you."

Poet

"Then why were you looking out the window?"

Actress

"You'd better tell me where you've dragged me to, you seducer!"

Poet

"But child, this was your idea. You wanted to go to the country-side—and specifically here."

Actress

"Well, wasn't I right?"

Poet

"Certainly. It's enchanting here. When you think about it—two hours from Vienna and complete solitude. And what countryside!"

Actress

"What? You could probably compose all sorts of things here, if you happened to have talent."

Poet

"Have you been here before?"

Actress

"Have I been here before? Ha! I lived here for years!"

Poet

"With whom?"

Actress

"With Fritz, naturally."

Poet

"Ah, I see."

Actress

"I absolutely worshipped that man!"

Poet

"You've already told me that."

Actress

"Please—I can leave again if I'm boring you!"

Poet

"You boring me? You have no idea what you mean to me. You are a world unto yourself. You are the divine, you are genius. You are... You are actually sacred simplicity itself. Yes, you. But you shouldn't be talking about Fritz now."

Actress

"That was certainly an aberration! Well!"

Poet

"It's beautiful that you recognize that."

Actress

"Come here, give me a kiss!"

The Poet kissed her.

Actress

"Now we should say goodnight to each other! Farewell, my darling!"

Poet

"What do you mean by that?"

Actress

"Well, I'm going to sleep!"

Poet

"Yes—that's fine, but as for saying goodnight... Where am I supposed to spend the night?"

Actress

"There are certainly many more rooms in this house."

Poet

"But the others hold no charm for me. I should light a lamp now, don't you think?"

Actress

"Yes."

The Poet lit the lamp that stood on the nightstand. Warm light flickered across the simple room.

Poet

"What a pretty room. And the people here are devout. Nothing but pictures of saints. It would be interesting to spend time among these people... quite another world. We really know so little about others."

Actress

"Stop talking nonsense and hand me that bag from the table instead."

Poet

"Here, my only one!"

The Actress took a small, framed picture from the little bag and placed it on the nightstand.

Poet

"What is that?"

Actress

"That's the Madonna."

Poet

"Do you always carry her with you?"

Actress

"She's my talisman. And now go, Robert!"

Poet

"But what kind of joke is this? Shouldn't I help you?"

Actress

"No, you should go now."

Poet

"And when should I come back?"

Actress

"In ten minutes."

The Poet kissed her.

Poet

"Until we meet again!"

Actress

"Where are you going?"

Poet

"I'll walk up and down outside your window. I love strolling outdoors at night. My best thoughts come to me that way. And especially near you, breathing in your longing, so to speak... weaving in your art."

Actress

"You talk like an idiot."

Poet

Pain flickered across his features.

"There are women who might say... like a poet."

Actress

"Now go already. But don't start an affair with the serving girl."

The Poet left. The Actress undressed, hearing his footsteps descend the wooden stairs and then pace beneath her window. Once she had undressed, she went to the window and looked down. He stood there in the moonlight. She called down in a whisper.

Actress

"Come!"

The Poet rushed back upstairs and burst toward her. She had slipped into bed and extinguished the light. He locked the door behind him.

Actress

"Now you can sit beside me and tell me something."

The Poet sat on the edge of the bed.

Poet

"Should I close the window? Aren't you cold?"

Actress

"Oh no!"

Poet

"What should I tell you?"

Actress

"Well, who are you being unfaithful to at this moment?"

Poet

"Unfortunately, I'm not being unfaithful yet."

Actress

"Well, console yourself. I'm also betraying someone."

Poet

"I can imagine that."

Actress

"And who do you think it is?"

Poet

"Child, I couldn't have any idea about that."

Actress

"Well, guess."

Poet

"Wait... Well, your director."

Actress

"My dear, I'm not a chorus girl."

Poet

"Well, I just thought..."

Actress

"Guess again."

Poet

"So you're betraying your colleague... Benno—"

Actress

"Ha! That man doesn't love women at all... don't you know that? That man has an affair with his postman!"

Poet

"Is that possible?"

Actress

"Just give me a kiss instead!"

The Poet embraced her.

Actress

"But what are you doing?"

Poet

"Don't torment me so."

Actress

"Listen, Robert, I'll make you a proposal. Get into bed with me."

Poet

"Accepted!"

Actress

"Come quickly, come quickly!"

Poet

"Yes... if it had been up to me, I would have been here long ago... Do you hear...?"

He held a hand up to his ear.

Actress

"What?"

Poet

"The crickets chirping outside."

Actress

"You must be mad, my child. There are no crickets here."

Poet

"But you can hear them."

Actress

"Now come, finally!"

Poet

"Here I am."

He moved to her.

Actress

"Now stay nice and still... Shh... don't move."

Poet

"What's gotten into you?"

Actress

"You'd really like to have an affair with me, wouldn't you?"

Poet

"That should already be clear to you."

Actress

"Well, many men would like that..."

Poet

"But there's no doubt that at this moment I have the best chances."

Actress

"Come then, my cricket! I'll call you Cricket from now on."

Poet

"Beautiful..."

Actress

"Now, who am I betraying?"

Poet

"Who? Perhaps myself..."

Actress

"My child, you're severely brain-damaged."

Poet

"Or someone... whom you've never seen... someone you don't know, someone who is destined for you and whom you can never find..."

Actress

"Please, don't talk so foolishly like a fairy tale."

Poet

"Isn't it strange... even you—and one would think... But no, it would rob you of your best if one wanted to... come, come—come—"

Actress

"This is more beautiful than acting in stupid plays... don't you think?"

Poet

"Well, I think it's good that you occasionally get to perform in sensible ones."

Actress

"You arrogant dog, you're surely thinking of your own again?"

Poet

"Absolutely!"

Actress (earnestly)

"It must be a magnificent piece!"

Poet

"Well then!"

Actress

"Yes, you are a great genius, Robert!"

Poet

"On this occasion, you could tell me why you cancelled the day before yesterday. There was absolutely nothing wrong with you."

Actress

"Well, I wanted to annoy you."

Poet

"But why? What had I done to you?"

Actress

"You were arrogant."

Poet

"How so?"

Actress

"Everyone at the theatre thinks so."

Poet

"I see."

Actress

"But I told them: The man has every right to be arrogant."

Poet

"And what did the others answer?"

Actress

"What should people answer me? I don't speak to any of them."

Poet

"Ah, I see."

Actress

"They would all love to poison me. But they won't succeed."

Poet

"Don't think about other people now. Be happy that we're here and tell me that you love me."

Actress

"Do you need further proof?"

Poet

"That can't be proven at all."

Actress

"That's wonderful! What more do you want?"

Poet

"How many have you wanted to prove it to in this way... did you love them all?"

Actress

"Oh no. I've only loved one."

Poet (embracing her)

"My..."

Actress

"Fritz."

Poet

"My name is Robert. What am I to you if you're thinking of Fritz now?"

Actress

"You are a whim."

Poet

"Good that I know it."

Actress

"Now tell me, aren't you proud?"

Poet

"Why should I be proud?"

Actress

"I think you have good reason to be."

Poet

"Ah, because of that."

Actress

"Yes, because of that, my pale cricket! Now, what about the chirping? Are they still chirping?"

Poet

"Continuously. Don't you hear it?"

Actress

"Of course, I hear it. But those are frogs, my child."

Poet

"You're mistaken; they croak."

Actress

"Certainly they croak."

Poet

"But not here, my child, here they chirp."

Actress

"You are probably the most stubborn thing I've ever encountered. Give me a kiss, my frog!"

Poet

"Please, don't call me that. It makes me downright nervous."

Actress

"Well, what should I call you?"

Poet

"I do have a name: Robert."

Actress

"Oh, that's too stupid."

Poet

"But I ask you to simply call me by my name."

Actress

"So Robert, give me a kiss... Ah!"

She kissed him.

"Are you satisfied now, frog? Hahahaha."

Poet

"Would you allow me to light a cigarette?"

Actress

"Give me one too."

He took the cigarette case from the nightstand, removed two cigarettes, lit both, and gave her one.

Actress

"By the way, you haven't said a word about my performance yesterday."

Poet

"What performance?"

Actress

"Well."

Poet

"Ah, yes. I wasn't at the theatre."

Actress

"You must be joking."

Poet

"Not at all. After you cancelled the day before yesterday, I assumed you still wouldn't be in full possession of your powers yesterday, so I preferred to stay away."

Actress

"You missed quite a lot."

Poet

"Is that so?"

Actress

"It was sensational. People turned pale."

Poet

"Did you notice that clearly?"

Actress

"Benno said: Child, you performed like a goddess."

Poet

"Hmm! But the day before yesterday, you were still so sick."

Actress

"Yes, I was. And do you know why? From longing for you."

Poet

"Earlier, you told me you wanted to annoy me, and that's why you cancelled."

Actress

"But what do you know of my love for you? It all leaves you cold. And I've been lying awake nights in fever, forty degrees!"

Poet

"For a whim, that's quite high."

Actress

"You call that a whim? I'm dying of love for you, and you call it a whim?!"

Poet

"And Fritz...?"

Actress

"Fritz? Don't speak to me of that galley slave!"

The moonlight streamed through the window, casting shadows across their intertwined forms. The Actress drew deeply on her cigarette, the ember glowing red in the darkness. Her theatrical gestures seemed amplified in the intimate space, each movement deliberate yet natural.

The Poet studied her profile in the pale light. Even here, away from the stage, she commanded attention with an intensity that both fascinated and unsettled him. Her ability to shift between passion and dismissal, between vulnerability and calculation, reminded him why he found actresses so compelling yet so dangerous to know.

Outside, the night sounds continued their chorus. Whether crickets or frogs, their rhythm provided a constant backdrop to the conversation that danced between affection and combat, sincerity and performance.

The Actress turned toward him, her eyes catching the moonlight.

Chapter Notes:

1. **Country inn**: Rural inns served as romantic retreats for Viennese couples seeking privacy away from the city's social surveillance. These establishments often offered rooms by the night to travelers and locals alike.

2. **Two hours from Vienna**: The distance suggests they traveled by train to a village in the Vienna Woods (Wienerwald), a popular destination for day trips and romantic escapes from urban life.

3. **Can't you see that I'm praying?**: The Actress's sudden turn to prayer reflects the complex relationship between sexuality and spirituality in Catholic Austria, where religious devotion coexisted with theatrical and bohemian lifestyles.

4. **I'm no pale scoundrel**: Her indignant response suggests that

atheism or religious skepticism was associated with moral corruption, particularly among intellectual and artistic circles.

5. **It won't make a pearl fall from your crown**: A metaphorical expression meaning prayer won't diminish his masculine dignity or intellectual superiority—addressing the poet's likely skepticism about religious observance.

6. **Libertine!**: A term for someone who pursues sexual pleasure without moral restraint, originally associated with 17th-18th century French aristocratic culture but commonly used to describe sexually adventurous men.

7. **I was praying to you**: The Actress's dramatic revelation transforms religious devotion into romantic worship, typical of the theatrical personality's tendency to dramatize emotions and blur sacred and profane love.

8. **Where you've dragged me to**: Despite having proposed the trip herself, the Actress now presents herself as seduced and led astray, reflecting the era's complex negotiations around female sexual agency.

9. **If you happened to have talent**: The Actress's cutting remark about the poet's abilities reveals the competitive and often cruel dynamics between artistic personalities, each seeking to establish superiority.

10. **With Fritz, naturally**: Fritz appears to be the Actress's former lover, suggesting she has a pattern of romantic retreats to this same location—making it both sentimental and practical for

her.

11. **I absolutely worshipped that man**: The intensity of her past devotion contrasts with her dismissive attitude toward Robert, suggesting her capacity for dramatic emotional attachments and reversals.

12. **You are a world unto yourself**: Robert's exaggerated compliments reflect the poet's tendency toward grandiose romantic language and his attempt to compete with her memories of Fritz.

13. **Sacred simplicity**: The same phrase Robert used about the Sweet Girl in the previous chapter, revealing his formulaic approach to flattering women and his limited vocabulary of romantic idealization.

14. **That was certainly an aberration**: The Actress's dismissal of her relationship with Fritz as a mistake shows her ability to rewrite her emotional history to suit present circumstances.

15. **Pictures of saints**: Religious imagery was common in Austrian rural inns, reflecting the deeply Catholic culture outside Vienna's more secular artistic circles. The contrast emphasizes their urban sophistication.

16. **Madonna**: A small framed picture of the Virgin Mary that the Actress carries as a talisman, showing how theatrical people often maintained personal religious practices alongside their unconventional lifestyles.

17. **Talisman**: An object believed to bring good luck or protection.

The Actress's Madonna serves both spiritual and superstitious functions, typical of theatrical people's blend of faith and folk belief.

18. **My best thoughts come to me that way**: The poet's claim that he composes while walking reflects the Romantic tradition of seeking inspiration in nature and solitude, a common artistic pose of the era.

19. **Breathing in your longing... weaving in your art**: Robert's pretentious metaphors about artistic inspiration show his need to intellectualize and poeticize every experience, even seduction.

20. **Don't start an affair with the serving girl**: The Actress's warning reveals her awareness of class and sexual hierarchies, as well as her possessive attitude toward Robert despite her own emotional inconsistency.

21. **There are women who might say... like a poet**: Robert's wounded response to being called an idiot shows his sensitivity about his artistic identity and his need for recognition as a serious writer.

22. **Cricket**: The Actress's pet name for Robert, derived from his earlier comment about hearing crickets outside, transforms his romantic observation into something diminutive and slightly mocking.

23. **You're severely brain-damaged**: Her harsh assessment of his romantic philosophizing reflects the Actress's impatience with

intellectual pretension and her preference for direct emotional expression.

24. **Someone who is destined for you**: Robert's mystical language about predestined love reflects late Romantic literary conventions about soulmates and spiritual connection that the Actress finds ridiculous.

25. **Don't talk so foolishly like a fairy tale**: Her dismissal of his romantic idealism shows the tension between theatrical artifice (which she controls) and literary romanticism (which he attempts to impose).

CHAPTER 9: THE ACTRESS AND THE COUNT

THE ACTRESS'S BEDROOM DISPLAYED an opulent arrangement of furniture and fabrics. Though noon had struck, the blinds remained drawn tight against the day. A single candle flickered on the nightstand, casting dancing shadows across the four-poster bed where the actress lay beneath silk coverlets. Numerous newspapers were scattered across the bedding like fallen leaves.

The Count entered wearing the uniform of a dragoon cavalry captain. He paused at the threshold, allowing his eyes to adjust to the dim interior.

Actress

"Ah, Count."

Count

"Your mother gave me permission, otherwise I wouldn't have—"

Actress

"Please, come closer."

Count

"I kiss your hand. Pardon me—coming in from the street like this... I can barely see anything yet. So... here we are. I kiss your hand."

The Count approached the bed, his spurs clicking softly against the Persian carpet. The scent of perfume and wilted flowers hung heavy in the warm air.

Actress

"Take a seat, Count."

Count

"Your mother told me you're indisposed... I hope it's nothing serious."

Actress

"Nothing serious? I was near death!"

Count

"Good God, how is that possible?"

Actress

"It's very kind of you to trouble yourself to visit me."

Count

"Near death! And last night you still performed like a goddess."

Actress

"It was quite a triumph."

Count

"Colossal! The audience was completely transported. And I won't even speak of myself."

Actress

"I thank you for the beautiful flowers."

Count

"Please, miss."

Actress

"There they stand."

She gestured with her eyes toward a large flower basket positioned on a small table by the window. The blooms, though still fragrant, showed signs of wilting in the closed room's stifling atmosphere.

Count

"You were positively showered with flowers and wreaths yesterday."

Actress

"All that still lies in my dressing room. Only your basket did I bring home with me."

Count

"That's sweet of you."

He bent to kiss her hand, but she suddenly took his and pressed it to her lips.

Count

"But miss."

Actress

"Don't be frightened, Count, this obligates you to nothing."

Count

"You are a strange creature... one might almost say enigmatic."

A pause settled between them, filled only by the distant sounds of Vienna beyond the shuttered windows.

Actress

"Miss Birken is probably easier to solve."

Count

"Yes, little Birken is no problem, although... I only know her superficially."

Actress

"Ha!"

Count

"You can trust me on this. But here's the thing - you're quite captivating. I've always been drawn to women like you. It was such a pleasure seeing you perform yesterday - I can't believe it was my first time."

Actress

"Is that possible?"

Count

"Yes. Look, miss, it's so difficult with the theatre. I'm accustomed to dining late... so when one arrives, the best part is over. Isn't that right?"

Actress

"Then from now on you'll simply eat earlier."

Count

"Yes, I've thought of that too. Or not at all. Dining really isn't any pleasure."

Actress

"What pleasures do you still know, you silver fox?"

Count

"I ask myself that sometimes! But I'm not a silver fox. There must be another reason."

Actress

"Do you think so?"

Count

"Yes. Lulu says, for example, that I'm a philosopher. You know, miss, he means I think too much."

Actress

"Yes... thinking, that's the misfortune."

Count

"I have too much time, that's why I think. Please, miss, look, I thought to myself, if they transfer me to Vienna, it will be better. There's distraction here, stimulation. But fundamentally, it's no different than up there."

Actress

"Where is this 'up there'?"

Count

"Well, you know miss, in Hungary, in those little places where I was mostly stationed."

Actress

"What did you do in Hungary?"

Count

"Well, as I said, miss, service."

Actress

"Why did you stay in Hungary so long?"

Count

"That's just how it happens."

Actress

"One must go mad there."

Count

"Why? One actually has more to do than here. You know, miss, training recruits, breaking in horses... and the countryside isn't as terrible as people say. The plain is quite beautiful—and such sunsets, it's a shame I'm not a painter. I sometimes thought, if I were a painter, I would paint it. We had one with the regiment, a young Splany, who could do it. But what am I telling you such dull stories for, miss?"

Actress

"Oh, please, I'm royally amused."

Count

"You know, miss, one can chat with you, Lulu already told me that, and that's what one seldom finds."

Actress

"Well, certainly, in Hungary."

Count

"But in Vienna just the same! People are the same everywhere; where there are more, the crowd is just bigger, that's the whole difference. Tell me, miss, do you actually like people?"

Actress

"Like them? I hate them! I can't stand to see any of them! I never see anyone either. I'm always alone. No one enters this house."

Count

"You see, I thought that you were actually a misanthrope. That must often occur with art. When one lives in such higher regions... well, you have it good, you at least know why you live!"

Actress

"Who tells you that? I have no idea why I live!"

Count

"I beg you, miss—famous, celebrated—"

Actress

"Is that perhaps happiness?"

Count

"Happiness? Please, miss, there is no happiness. Generally, the very things that are talked about most don't exist at all... for example, love. That's also such a thing."

Actress

"You're probably right."

Count

"Pleasure... intoxication... well, there's nothing to say against that... that's something certain. Now I'm enjoying myself... good, I know I'm enjoying myself. Or I'm intoxicated, fine. That's also certain. And when it's over, then it's simply over."

Actress

"It is over!"

Her voice carried a theatrical grandeur that seemed to fill the dim room.

Count

"But as soon as one doesn't—how should I express myself—as soon as one doesn't surrender to the moment, I mean thinks about later or about earlier... well, it's immediately finished. Later is sad... earlier is uncertain... in a word... one only becomes confused. Am I not right?"

Actress

"You have grasped the meaning."

She nodded with wide eyes, studying his face in the candlelight.

Count

"And you see, miss, once that has become clear to someone, it's quite the same whether one lives in Vienna or in the Puszta or in Steinamanger. Look, for example... where may I put my cap? So, thank you kindly... what were we just talking about?"

Actress

"About Steinamanger."

Count

"Right. So as I said, the difference isn't great. Whether I sit in the casino in the evening or in the club, it's all the same."

Actress

"And how does this relate to love?"

Count

"If one believes in it, there's always one who likes you."

Actress

"For example, Miss Birken."

Count

"I really don't know, miss, why you always bring up little Birken."

Actress

"She's your mistress."

Count

"Who says that?"

Actress

"Every person knows that."

Count

"Only I don't, it's peculiar."

Actress

"You fought a duel over her!"

Count

"Perhaps I was even shot dead and didn't notice it."

Actress

"Well, Count, you are a man of honor. Sit closer."

Count

"I take the liberty."

Actress

"Here."

She pulled him toward her, running her hand through his hair. The gesture was both tender and possessive, her fingers catching briefly on the pomade that held his military bearing even in this intimate setting.

"I knew that you would come today!"

Count

"How so?"

Actress

"I already knew it yesterday in the theatre."

Count

"Did you see me from the stage?"

Actress

"Definitely! Didn't you notice that I was playing only for you?"

Count

"How is that possible?"

Actress

"I was so inspired when I saw you sitting in the front row!"

Count

"Inspired? Because of me? I had no idea that you noticed me!"

Actress

"You can drive one to despair with your refinement."

Count

"Yes, miss..."

Actress

"'Yes, miss!'... At least unbuckle your sabre!"

Count

"If it's permitted."

He unbuckled the weapon and leaned it against the bed, the metal catching the candlelight with a brief gleam.

Actress

"And finally give me a kiss."

Count

He kissed her, but she held him close and wouldn't let him go.

Actress

"I should never have laid eyes on you either."

Count

"It's better this way!"

Actress

"Count, you are a poseur!"

Count

"I—why?"

Actress

"What do you think, how happy many a man would be if he could be in your place!"

Count

"I am very happy."

Actress

"Well, I thought there was no happiness. How are you looking at me? I believe you're afraid of me, Count!"

Count

"I told you, miss, you are a problem."

Actress

"Oh, leave me in peace with philosophy... come to me. And now ask me for something... you can have everything you want. You are too beautiful."

Count

"So I ask permission to return this evening."

He kissed her hand as he spoke, his military bearing softening in the intimate atmosphere.

Actress

"This evening... but I'm performing."

Count

"After the theatre."

Actress

"You don't ask for anything else?"

Count

"For everything else, I will ask after the theatre."

Actress

"Then you can ask for a long time, you wretched poseur."

The hurt in her voice was genuine beneath the theatrical delivery.

Count

"Yes, look, or look here, we've been so honest with each other until now... I would find it all much more beautiful in the evening after the theatre... more comfortable than now, when... I always have the feeling that the door could open..."

Actress

"It doesn't open from the outside."

Count

"Look, I think one shouldn't carelessly spoil something from the start that could possibly be very beautiful."

Actress

"Possibly!"

Count

"In the morning, if I'm to tell the truth, I find love horrible."

Actress

"Well—you are probably the most insane thing that has ever happened to me!"

Count

"I'm not talking about any random women... after all, in general, it doesn't matter. But women like you... no, you can call me a fool a hundred times. But women like you... one doesn't take before breakfast."

Actress

"God, how sweet you are!"

Count

"Do you understand what I said, don't you. I imagine it like this—"

Actress

"Well, how do you imagine it?"

Count

"I think... I wait for you after the theatre in a carriage, then we drive somewhere together to have supper—"

Actress

"I am not Miss Birken."

Count

"I didn't say that. I just think that everything requires mood. I only get in the mood during supper. That's the most beautiful part, when one drives home together from supper, then..."

Actress

"What is then?"

Count

"Well then... that lies in the development of things."

Actress

"Do sit closer. Closer."

Count

He seated himself on the bed. "I must say, from the cushions comes such a... that's reseda, isn't it?"

Actress

"It's very hot here, don't you think?"

The Count leaned down and kissed her neck, tasting the salt of perspiration mixed with her perfume.

Actress

"Oh, Count, that's against your program."

Count

"Who says that? I have no program."

She pulled him closer to her, her hands working at the buttons of his uniform jacket.

Count

"It really is hot."

Actress

"Do you think so? And so dark, as if it were evening..."

She pulled him against her with sudden intensity.

"It is evening... it is night... Close your eyes if it's too bright for you. Come! Come!"

The Count no longer resisted, surrendering to the moment as the afternoon light filtered weakly through the heavy curtains, casting their entwined forms in amber shadows.

Actress

"Well, how is it now with the mood, you poseur?"

Count

"You are a little devil."

Actress

"What kind of expression is that?"

Count

"Well, then an angel."

Actress

"And you should have become an actor! Truly! You know women! And do you know what I'm going to do now?"

Count

"Well?"

Actress

"I'm going to tell you that I never want to see you again."

Count

"Why?"

Actress

"No, no. You're too dangerous for me! You drive a woman mad. Now you suddenly stand before me as if nothing had happened."

She pulled the silk sheet around herself, her hair cascading over her bare shoulders in waves that caught the filtered afternoon light. The Count adjusted his uniform, his movements controlled despite the intimacy they had just shared.

Count

"But..."

Actress

"I ask you to remember, Count, I have just been your lover."

Count

"I'll never forget it!"

The words carried a weight that surprised even him. He fastened the buttons of his jacket, though his hands trembled slightly.

Actress

"And what about tonight?"

Count

"What do you mean?"

Actress

"Well—you wanted to wait for me after the theatre?"

She stretched languidly against the pillows, watching him with calculating eyes. The bedroom felt heavy with the scent of their encounter and her perfume, a cloying sweetness that seemed to cling to everything.

Count

"Yes, well then, the day after tomorrow."

Actress

"What does that mean, the day after tomorrow? We were talking about today."

Count

"That wouldn't make proper sense."

Actress

"You old man!"

The accusation stung more than he expected. He straightened his shoulders, the military bearing returning as if it were armor against her words.

Count

"You don't understand me properly. I mean that more, what, how should I express myself, what concerns the soul."

Actress

"What do I care about your soul?"

Count

"Believe me, it belongs to it. I consider it a false view that one can separate such things from each other."

He moved to the window, pulling back the heavy curtain slightly. The afternoon sun streamed in, revealing dust motes dancing in the air and the rumpled state of the bedsheets. The contrast between the ordered world outside and the chaos of passion within struck him forcefully.

Actress

"Leave me in peace with your philosophy. When I want that, I'll read a book."

Count

"One never really learns from books."

Actress

"That's probably true! That's why you should wait for me tonight. We'll come to an agreement about the soul, you scoundrel!"

She sat up in bed, the sheet falling away from her shoulders. Her eyes blazed with a mixture of desire and defiance that made his carefully constructed reserve waver.

Count

"So if you permit, I will come with my carriage..."

Actress

"You will wait for me here in my apartment—"

Count

"—After the theatre."

Actress

"Naturally."

He moved to where his sabre leaned against the bed, the metal cool under his fingers as he lifted it. The weight of the weapon felt reassuring, a reminder of his world beyond this perfumed chamber.

Actress

"What are you doing?"

Count

"I think it's time that I go. For a courtesy visit, I've actually stayed a bit too long already."

He buckled the sabre around his waist, the leather creaking softly in the quiet room. The familiar ritual helped restore his sense of propriety, though the memory of her touch still burned on his skin.

Actress

"Well, tonight it won't be a courtesy visit."

Count

"Do you not think so?"

Actress

"Just let me take care of that. And now give me another kiss, my little philosopher. There, you seducer, you... sweet child, you soul-seller, you polecat, you..."

She pulled him down to her with sudden fierce intensity, her lips finding his in a series of passionate kisses that left him breathless. Her hands tangled in his hair, messing the careful arrangement he had restored. Then, just as suddenly, she pushed him away with force that sent him stumbling backward.

"Count, it was a great honor!"

The dismissal was theatrical yet genuine, delivered with the same commanding presence she no doubt brought to the stage. He straightened his uniform once more, his composure returning like a mask sliding into place.

Count

"I kiss your hand, Miss!"

He moved toward the door, his boots clicking against the polished floor. At the threshold, he turned back briefly, taking in the sight of her surrounded by silk and shadows.

"Until we meet again."

Actress

"Farewell, Steinamanger!"

The nickname followed him as he closed the door behind him, leaving her alone in the dimly lit bedroom where the afternoon light continued to fade through the heavy curtains.

Chapter Notes:

1. **Opulent arrangement of furniture and fabrics**: The Actress's bedroom reflects the wealth and status that successful stage performers could achieve in late 19th-century Vienna, when popular actresses were among the few women who could earn independent fortunes.

2. **Noon had struck, the blinds remained drawn**: Keeping rooms dark during midday was common among theatrical people who worked evenings and slept late, but also suggests the languid, sensual lifestyle associated with actresses.

3. **Four-poster bed**: An expensive furniture piece associated with wealth and an aristocratic lifestyle. For an actress to own such a bed demonstrated her financial success and social aspirations.

4. **Dragoon cavalry captain**: Elite cavalry officers in the Austrian army, typically from aristocratic families. Dragoons were mounted infantry who fought both on horseback and on foot, considered prestigious military units.

5. **Your mother gave me permission**: Respectable visiting protocol required permission from a chaperone or family member.

The Count's formal approach shows his adherence to social proprieties even in this intimate situation.

6. **I kiss your hand**: The standard formal greeting between a gentleman and lady in Austrian society, emphasizing respect and maintaining social distance even in private settings.

7. **Spurs clicking softly**: Cavalry officers wore spurs as part of their uniform even when not riding. The sound emphasizes his military bearing and the formality he brings to this intimate encounter.

8. **Persian carpet**: An expensive luxury item indicating the Actress's wealth and refined taste. Persian rugs were highly prized status symbols in European homes.

9. **You were positively showered with flowers**: Throwing flowers and wreaths onto the stage was how audiences showed appreciation for performers. Successful actresses could receive dozens of floral tributes after a popular performance.

10. **Miss Birken**: Another actress who apparently has a relationship with the Count. The casual mention reveals the social network of relationships between aristocratic men and theatrical women.

11. **Silver fox**: Austrian slang for an older man who is still attractive to women. The Count's sensitivity to being called this suggests anxiety about aging and sexual attractiveness.

12. **Lulu**: The Count's friend or fellow officer, whose nickname suggests aristocratic social circles where men were known by

informal names or military nicknames.

13. **Philosopher**: The accusation that he "thinks too much" reflects the stereotype of aristocratic ennui and the supposed burden of education and leisure time among the upper classes.

14. **Transfer me to Vienna**: Military officers were often stationed in remote garrison towns throughout the Austro-Hungarian Empire. Transfer to Vienna was considered a plum assignment offering social and cultural opportunities.

15. **Hungary**: Part of the Austro-Hungarian Empire where many Austrian officers served in garrison duty. Rural Hungarian postings were considered boring and culturally isolated compared to Vienna.

16. **Training recruits, breaking in horses**: Standard duties for cavalry officers in remote postings. The Count's description emphasizes the routine, unglamorous aspects of military service away from the capital.

17. **Young Splany**: A fellow officer with artistic abilities, possibly Czech or Slavic based on the surname. Many officers came from various ethnic groups within the multi-ethnic Austrian Empire.

18. **The plain**: The Hungarian puszta (Great Plain), a vast grassland region known for its dramatic landscapes and spectacular sunsets that inspired many Austrian and Hungarian artists.

19. **Famous, celebrated**: The Actress's theatrical success has brought her public recognition and wealth, making her one

of Vienna's celebrity figures and thus attractive to aristocratic admirers.

20. **Puszta**: The Hungarian Great Plain, characterized by vast open grasslands and dramatic skies. Austrian officers stationed there often found it either inspiring or depressingly monotonous.

21. **Steinamanger**: A real town in western Hungary (now Szombathely) where Austrian regiments were commonly stationed. The name became the Actress's mocking nickname for the Count, emphasizing his provincial military background.

22. **Casino**: Military officers' social clubs found in garrison towns throughout the Empire, providing dining, gaming, and social interaction for the officer class stationed away from major cities.

23. **Club**: Exclusive gentlemen's clubs in Vienna where aristocratic and military men gathered for dining, conversation, and business. These were centers of male social and political life.

24. **Man of honor**: The formal code of conduct expected from aristocratic and military men, emphasizing integrity, courage, and adherence to social conventions—including discretion about romantic affairs.

25. **Sabre**: Standard weapon for cavalry officers, worn as part of the dress uniform. Unbuckling it represents both practical necessity and symbolic relaxation of military formality.

26. **Before breakfast**: The Count's philosophy that morning intimacy lacks proper romantic atmosphere reflects aristocratic ideas about appropriate timing for various social and romantic

activities.

27. **After the theatre**: Evening entertainment was the proper time for romantic encounters among the upper classes, allowing for elaborate rituals of dining, conversation, and gradual romantic progression.

28. **Reseda**: A plant whose flowers were used to make a popular perfume in the 19th century, known for its sweet, distinctive scent often associated with feminine elegance.

29. **Steinamanger**: The Actress's final dismissive nickname for the Count, reducing him to his provincial military posting and emphasizing her theatrical superiority over his aristocratic pretensions.

CHAPTER 10: THE COUNT AND THE PROSTITUTE

MORNING, AROUND SIX O'CLOCK.

A shabby room with a single window, where yellowed, grimy blinds hung lowered. Worn greenish curtains framed the glass. A dresser displayed a few photographs and a conspicuously tasteless, cheap lady's hat. Behind the mirror, cheap Japanese fans gathered dust.

On the table, covered with a reddish protective cloth, stood a petroleum lamp burning weakly with an acrid smell. Its paper yellow lampshade cast sickly light beside a jug containing beer dregs and a half-emptied glass.

On the floor beside the bed lay women's clothes in disarray, as if hastily thrown off. In the bed slept the prostitute, breathing peacefully. On the divan, fully clothed in his drab overcoat, lay the Count. His hat rested on the floor at the head of the divan.

The Count stirred, rubbing his eyes before sitting up abruptly. He remained seated, looking around with confusion.

Count

"Yes, how did I... Ah, so... So I really did go home with this woman."

He stood quickly, glancing toward her bed where she lay unconscious to his presence.

"There she lies... What can still happen to a man at my age. I have no idea if they carried me up here? No... I saw it - I came into this room... yes... I was still awake then, or became awake... or... or is it perhaps only that this room reminds me of something? Upon my soul, well yes... yesterday I saw it... but..."

He checked his watch, the ticking unnaturally loud in the morning stillness.

"What! Yesterday, a few hours ago - But I knew something had to happen... I felt it... when I started drinking yesterday, I felt it, that... And what did happen? So nothing... Or is there something? Upon my soul... for... well, for ten years such a thing hasn't happened to me, that I don't know... In short, I was simply drunk. If only I knew from when... Well, I remember quite clearly how I went into that brothel café with Lulu and... no, no... we left Sacher's... and then on the way already... Yes, right, I rode in my carriage with Lulu... Why am I racking my brains so much. It doesn't matter. Let's see about getting away."

He stood up, causing the lamp to wobble precariously on its base.

"Oh!"

His eyes fixed on the sleeping woman, her face peaceful in the dim light.

"She certainly has a healthy sleep. I don't know anything about anything - but I'll put the money on the nightstand... and goodbye."

He moved closer, studying her features in the lamplight. The shadows played across her face, softening the harsh lines that daylight would reveal.

"If one didn't know what she is!"

He continued to observe her for a long moment, something stirring in his chest that he couldn't quite name.

"I've known many who haven't looked so virtuous even while sleeping. Upon my soul... well, Lulu would say again that I philosophize, but it's true, sleep makes one look, it seems to me - like the brother, well, death... Hmm, I'd just like to know whether... No, I would have to remember that... No, no, I fell right onto this divan... and nothing happened... It's unbelievable how sometimes all women look similar... Well, let's go."

He moved toward the door, then paused, remembering something essential. Taking out his wallet, he began to extract a banknote when a voice interrupted him.

Prostitute

"Well... who's there so early in the morning?"

She recognized him as consciousness returned, her voice thick with sleep.

"Hello, darling!"

Count

"Good morning. Did you sleep well?"

Prostitute

"Ah, come here. Give me a kiss."

Count

The Count bent toward her, then thought better of it and pulled back.

"I was just about to leave..."

Prostitute

"Leave?"

Count

"It really is high time."

Prostitute

"So you want to leave?"

Count

The question made him almost embarrassed, as if caught in some impropriety.

"Well..."

Prostitute

"Well, goodbye then; come back another time."

Count

"Yes, God bless you. Well, won't you give me your hand?"

The prostitute extended her hand from beneath the covers. He took it and kissed it mechanically, then noticed what he was doing and laughed.

Like a princess. Besides, if one only...

Prostitute

"Why are you looking at me like that?"

Count

"If one only sees the little head, like now... when waking up, every woman looks innocent... upon my soul, one could imagine all sorts of things, if it didn't stink so much of petroleum..."

Prostitute

"Yes, there's always trouble with that lamp."

Count

"How old are you actually?"

Prostitute

"Well, what do you think?"

Count

"Twenty-four."

Prostitute

"Yes, of course."

Count

"Are you older?"

Prostitute

"I'm going into my twentieth year."

Count

"And how long have you been..."

Prostitute

"I've been in this business for one year!"

Count

"Then you started quite early."

Prostitute

"Better too early than too late."

The Count sat on the edge of the bed, the mattress sagging under his weight. The morning light filtering through the grimy blinds cast everything in sepia tones.

Count

"Tell me something, are you actually happy?"

Prostitute

"What?"

Count

"Well, I mean, are things going well for you?"

Prostitute

"Oh, things always go well for me."

Count

"I see... Tell me, has it never occurred to you that you could become something else?"

Prostitute

"What should I become?"

Count

"Well... You're really a pretty girl. You could, for example, have a lover."

Prostitute

"You think maybe I don't have one?"

Count

"Yes, I know that - but I mean one, you know, *one* who would keep you, so you wouldn't have to go with just anyone."

Prostitute

"I don't go with just anyone either. Thank God, I don't have to do that; I choose for myself."

The Count looked around the room, taking in the shabby furnishings and peeling wallpaper with new eyes.

The prostitute noticed his scrutiny.

"Next month we're moving into the city, to Spiegelgasse."

Count

"We? Who?"

Prostitute

"Well, the madam, and the couple of other girls who still live here."

Count

"There are still others living here—"

Prostitute

"Right next door... don't you hear... that's Milli, who was also in the café."

Count

"Someone's snoring."

Prostitute

"That's Milli already; she snores the whole day through until ten at night. Then she gets up and goes to the café."

Count

"That's a dreadful life."

Prostitute

"Of course. The madam gets angry enough about it. I'm always on the streets by noon."

Count

"What do you do on the streets at noon?"

Prostitute

"What would I do? I go on the beat."

Count

"Ah, yes... naturally..."

He stood up, taking out his wallet and placing a banknote on the nightstand with deliberate care.

"Farewell!"

Prostitute

"Going already... Goodbye... Come back soon."

She turned onto her side, already half-asleep again. The Count paused at the door, something unresolved gnawing at him.

Count

"Tell me something, everything's all the same to you - isn't it?"

Prostitute

"What?"

Count

"I mean, it doesn't give you any pleasure anymore."

Prostitute

She yawned, stretching like a cat in the tangled sheets.

"I'm so sleepy."

Count

"It's all the same to you whether someone is young or old or whether someone..."

Prostitute

"What are you asking?"

Count

The realization struck him suddenly, like a physical blow.

"Well... upon my soul, now I know who you remind me of, that is..."

Prostitute

"Do I look like someone?"

Count

"Unbelievable, unbelievable, now I ask you very much, don't say anything at all, for at least a minute..."

He stared at her intently, his breath catching in his throat.

"Exactly the same face, exactly the same face."

He kissed her suddenly on the eyes, a gesture tender and desperate.

Prostitute

"Well..."

Count

"Upon my soul, it's a pity that you... aren't something else... You could make your fortune!"

Prostitute

"You're just like Franz."

Count

"Who is Franz?"

Prostitute

"Well, the waiter from our café..."

Count

"How am I just like Franz?"

Prostitute

"He also always says I could make my fortune and I should marry him."

Count

"Why don't you do it?"

Prostitute

"Thank you very much... I don't want to marry, no, not for any price. Later perhaps."

Count

"The eyes... exactly the eyes... Lulu would surely say I'm a fool - but I want to kiss your eyes once more... like this... and now God bless you, now I'm going."

Prostitute

"Goodbye..."

At the door, the Count turned back one final time.

Count

"You... tell me... doesn't it surprise you at all..."

Prostitute

"What?"

Count

"That I want nothing from you."

Prostitute

"There are many men who aren't in the mood in the morning."

Count

"Well, yes..."

He spoke to himself, struggling with some internal conflict.

"Too stupid that I want her to be surprised... Well, goodbye..."

He reached the door, then stopped again.

"Actually, I'm annoyed with myself. I know that such women only care about money... what am I saying - such... it's nice... that she at least doesn't pretend, that should rather please one... You - you know, I'll come back to you soon."

Prostitute

Her eyes were already closed again.

"Good."

Count

"When are you always at home?"

Prostitute

"I'm always at home. You just need to ask for Leocadia."

Count

"Leocadia... Fine - Well, God bless you."

He paused at the door, wine still clouding his thoughts.

"I still have the wine in my head. Well, that's really the height... I'm with such a woman and have done nothing but kiss her eyes because she reminded me of someone..."

He turned back to her once more.

"You, Leocadia, does it happen to you often that someone leaves you like this?"

Prostitute

"How?"

Count

"Like me?"

Prostitute

"In the morning?"

Count

"No... whether someone has ever been with you - and wanted nothing from you?"

Prostitute

"No, that has never happened to me."

Count

"Well, what do you think? Do you think you don't appeal to me?"

Prostitute

"Why shouldn't I appeal to you? Last night I appealed to you."

Count

"You appeal to me now too."

Prostitute

"But last night I appealed to you better."

Count

"Why do you think that?"

Prostitute

"Well, why are you asking such stupid questions?"

Count

"Last night... yes, tell me, didn't I fall right onto the divan?"

Prostitute

"Well, of course... together with me."

Count

"With you?"

Prostitute

"Yes, don't you remember that anymore?"

Count

"I have... we were together... yes..."

Prostitute

"But you fell asleep right away."

Count

"Right away I... So... So that's how it was!"

Prostitute

"Yes, darling. But you must have had a proper drunk on, that you don't remember anymore."

Count

"So... And yet... there's a distant resemblance... Goodbye..."

He listened to sounds from beyond the room.

"What's going on?"

Prostitute

"The chambermaid is already up. Go on, give her something when you leave. The gate is also open; you'll save the doorkeeper."

Count

"Yes."

In the anteroom, he spoke to himself once more.

"Well... It would have been beautiful if I had only kissed her on the eyes. That would almost have been an adventure... It just wasn't meant for me."

The chambermaid appeared and opened the door for him.

"Ah - here you are... Good night."

Chambermaid

"Good morning."

Count

"Yes, of course... good morning... good morning."

Chapter Notes:

1. **Shabby room with a single window**: Typical accommodation for prostitutes in late 19th-century Vienna, often located in working-class districts with minimal furnishings and poor maintenance.

2. **Yellowed, grimy blinds**: Window coverings that have become discolored from smoke, poor ventilation, and lack of cleaning—indicating the room's low-rent status and neglect.

3. **Cheap Japanese fans**: Mass-produced decorative items that became popular in Europe during the late 1800s "Japonisme" craze, but here emphasizing their tasteless, inexpensive quality.

4. **Petroleum lamp**: Kerosene lamps were common lighting in lower-class accommodations that lacked gas or electric service. The "acrid smell" indicates poor-quality fuel or a dirty wick.

5. **Paper yellow lampshade**: Cheap colored paper shades were used to soften harsh petroleum light but often became fire hazards and added to the room's sickly atmosphere.

6. **Beer dregs**: The remnants of beer in glasses, suggesting recent drinking and the casual, lower-class atmosphere of the encounter.

7. **Drab overcoat**: Military or civilian overcoats of this period were typically gray or brown wool, practical but unglamorous garments worn by men of all social classes.

8. **Sacher's**: A famous luxury hotel and restaurant in Vienna, still operating today. Frequented by aristocrats and wealthy visitors,

it was known for its elegant atmosphere and famous Sacher-torte.

9. **Brothel café**: Establishments that served coffee and alcohol while facilitating prostitution, operating in a legal gray area in late 19th-century Vienna's regulated sex trade.

10. **Lulu**: The Count's aristocratic friend, previously mentioned in other chapters. Such nicknames were common among the Austrian officer class and nobility.

11. **Carriage**: Horse-drawn vehicles used by wealthy Viennese for transportation. Owning a private carriage was a significant mark of wealth and social status.

12. **Upon my soul**: A mild oath expressing sincerity or surprise, considered more refined than stronger language and typical of educated, upper-class speech.

13. **Nightstand**: The small table beside the bed where clients would typically leave payment for prostitutes, making the transaction appear less directly commercial.

14. **Spiegelgasse**: German for "Mirror Street," a real street name in Vienna. The prostitute's mention of moving there suggests upward mobility within the sex trade hierarchy.

15. **Madam**: The woman who managed a group of prostitutes, providing housing, protection, and clients in exchange for a percentage of earnings—a common business arrangement in regulated prostitution.

16. **On the beat**: Police and prostitution terminology for walking the streets looking for clients. "Working the beat" was the most dangerous and lowest-paid form of sex work.

17. **Franz**: The waiter from the café mentioned in earlier chapters, showing how characters' lives intersect across social boundaries in Schnitzler's Vienna.

18. **Leocadia**: An unusual name for a Viennese prostitute, possibly indicating foreign origins or an assumed professional identity. The name has Greek roots meaning "bright" or "clear."

19. **Wine in my head**: The Count's acknowledgment that alcohol clouded his judgment, reflecting the common experience of upper-class men who visited prostitutes while intoxicated.

20. **Chambermaid**: A servant who cleaned rooms and assisted guests in hotels and brothels. Her expectation of a tip shows the economic ecosystem surrounding prostitution.

21. **Gate is open**: Refers to the building's main entrance. Late at night, buildings were typically locked, requiring payment to doorkeepers for entry—another cost in the prostitution economy.

22. **Good morning**: The chambermaid's correction of the Count's "Good night" emphasizes his disorientation and the inversion of normal social rhythms in the world of commercial sex.

23. **Kissed her on the eyes**: Kissing someone's closed eyelids was considered an extremely intimate and tender gesture in 19th-century European culture, more romantic and spiritual

than sexual. This type of kiss suggested deep affection, reverence, or a desire to protect the person's innocence. The Count's repeated focus on Leocadia's eyes and his gentle kisses there reveal his genuine emotional confusion—he's treating a prostitute with the tenderness typically reserved for a beloved or pure woman, blurring the boundaries between commercial transaction and romantic feeling that his social class normally maintained strictly separate.

CHAPTER SUMMARIES AND ANALYSIS

CHAPTER I: "THE PROSTITUTE AND THE SOLDIER"

Summary and Plot Analysis

CHAPTER ONE PRESENTS A brief but psychologically complex encounter between Franz, an Austrian soldier, and Leocadia, a street prostitute, beginning near Vienna's Augarten Bridge on an evening in the late 19th century.

The narrative unfolds through three distinct phases: the initial street negotiation where Leocadia attempts to solicit Franz while he expresses both interest and reluctance due to time constraints and lack of money, the movement from public to private space as they descend to the secluded Danube embankment for their sexual encounter, and the brutal aftermath where Franz abandons Leocadia without payment despite her plea for "at least a sixpence for the caretaker."

The plot's apparent simplicity masks a sophisticated examination of urban alienation, class dynamics, and the commodification of human intimacy in imperial Vienna, with each phase revealing different aspects of how social structures shape the most intimate human interactions.

Technical Structure and Literary Technique

Schnitzler employs a theatrical, dialogue-driven technique that employs dramatic vignettes with minimal narrative intrusion. The chapter's three-scene structure mirrors classical dramatic progression, while the predominantly conversational format allows characters to reveal their psychology through speech patterns and word choices rather than authorial exposition.

The author's use of geographic movement—from the well-lit bridge through increasingly dark and isolated spaces to the riverbank—functions as both literal plot development and symbolic descent from public respectability to private transgression.

Schnitzler's sparse descriptive passages serve strategic purposes: the "amber glow" of gas lamps, Leocadia's "worn but clean" dress, and the "scent of cheap soap and something floral" create atmospheric realism while establishing the socioeconomic context without sentimentality.

The technique of dramatic compression, where an entire relationship cycle of attraction, consummation, and abandonment occurs within a single brief encounter, anticipates modernist approaches to narrative time while maintaining the clinical objectivity that characterizes naturalistic literature.

The author's medical training is evident in his detached, almost sociological observation of human behavior, presenting the encounter without moral judgment while allowing the social critique to emerge through the characters' actions and dialogue.

Social Class Dynamics and Urban Politics

The encounter illuminates the complex class stratifications of Habsburg Vienna, where Franz occupies a peculiar position as someone with symbolic authority (his sabre and uniform) but economic powerlessness (his lack of money and strict military curfew), while Leocadia represents the most economically vulnerable class yet possesses certain forms of agency within her limited sphere.

Her differentiated pricing structure—"The civilians pay me... Chaps like you don't have to pay me for anything"—reveals how the sexual economy operated along class lines, with prostitutes recognizing that soldiers, despite their uniforms and weapons, remained essentially working-class men with little disposable income.

Franz's comment about carrying a sabre in response to her warning about guards demonstrates how military authority functioned as both practical protection and psychological compensation for economic insecurity, while his ultimate refusal to pay reveals the particular exploitation faced by women who served men too poor to afford their services yet entitled enough to demand them.

The urban geography itself becomes a character in the social dynamics: the Augarten Bridge represents a liminal space where different classes intersect, while the descent to the riverbank symbolizes movement away from the regulated public sphere into spaces where social rules become fluid and exploitation more easily concealed.

Leocadia's superior knowledge of the city's hidden spaces—her confident navigation of the dark embankment and awareness of secluded locations—demonstrates how marginalized people develop expertise in urban geography that serves both survival and professional purposes.

Gender Relations and Sexual Politics

The sexual encounter reveals the profound gender asymmetries that structure relationships between men and women across all social classes in late imperial Austria.

Despite Leocadia's initial control of the interaction—she initiates contact, guides the negotiation, and leads Franz to the secluded location—the ultimate power dynamic becomes clear when Franz simply walks away without payment or acknowledgment, exercising a form of masculine privilege that transcends class boundaries.

Leocadia's attempt to transform the commercial transaction into something approaching emotional connection—"I like that best anyway—when I love someone"—exposes the psychological strategies women employed to preserve dignity within dehumanizing circumstances, while Franz's immediate emotional withdrawal demonstrates male patterns of sexual consumption that treat intimacy as purely physical gratification.

The encounter's aftermath, where Leocadia stands alone by the dark water while Franz disappears into the night, crystallizes the gendered nature of sexual vulnerability in urban modernity: women bear the physical and emotional consequences of sexual encounters while men retain mobility and freedom from obligation.

Her final curses—"Scoundrel! Bastard!"—represent not merely personal anger but a broader female protest against systemic male irresponsibility, though the words dissipate harmlessly into the night air, suggesting the powerlessness of such protests against entrenched social structures.

Historical Context and Cultural Commentary

For contemporary readers, several elements require historical explanation to fully appreciate Schnitzler's social critique.

The Augarten Bridge area was known in fin-de-siècle Vienna as a district where soldiers and working-class people congregated, making it a realistic setting for this type of encounter, while the gas lamp lighting creates the characteristic pools of illumination and shadow that structured urban nightlife before electric street lighting became widespread.

Franz's concern about the ten o'clock barracks curfew reflects the rigid discipline of Habsburg military life, where soldiers faced severe punishment for tardiness, making his time pressure genuine rather than merely an excuse for quick sexual gratification.

The mention of guards refers to military police who patrolled Vienna's streets to maintain order and ensure soldiers returned to barracks punctually, while Franz's sabre represents standard equipment for Austrian infantry that served both practical and symbolic functions as a marker of imperial authority.

Leocadia's unusual name—with its Greek origins meaning "bright" or "clear"—creates dramatic irony given her circumstances and possibly suggests foreign origins or an assumed professional identity, reflecting the cosmopolitan nature of imperial Vienna where people from across the empire sought economic opportunities.

The "sixpence for the caretaker" represents a common excuse prostitutes used to extract minimal payment, supposedly for bribing building superintendents who might otherwise report illicit activities, though in Leocadia's case it may simply represent a desperate attempt to receive some acknowledgment of the transaction's human cost.

Psychological Realism and Thematic Significance

Schnitzler's psychological penetration reveals how individual desires and needs become distorted by social structures that commodify human intimacy while maintaining facades of respectability and moral order.

Franz's behavior demonstrates the psychological contradictions faced by working-class men who possess symbolic authority through military service yet remain economically powerless, leading to compensatory assertions of masculine privilege through sexual exploitation of even more vulnerable women.

His immediate departure after the sexual encounter suggests not merely callousness but psychological discomfort with intimacy that threatens his self-conception as someone above the social level of his sexual partners.

Leocadia's attempt to create emotional connection within a commercial framework reveals the human need for dignity and recognition that persists even in the most degraded circumstances, while her professional knowledge of the city's hidden spaces demonstrates the survival skills developed by marginalized people who must navigate urban environments that are simultaneously spaces of opportunity and danger.

The chapter's integration into the larger "round dance" structure becomes apparent through Franz's reference to other women he has encountered, suggesting that this type of brief, unsatisfying encounter represents a recurring pattern rather than an isolated incident, creating chains of connection and abandonment that perpetuate social alienation rather than genuine human contact.

The encounter's ultimate failure to satisfy either participant—Franz gains physical gratification but no emotional connection, while Leocadia receives neither payment nor affection—illustrates Schnitzler's central theme about how modern urban life commodifies the most intimate human experiences, creating mechanical exchanges that leave all parties emotionally impoverished while maintaining the appearance of social interaction and sexual fulfillment.

CHAPTER 2: "THE SOLDIER AND THE PARLOUR MAID"

SUMMARY AND PLOT ANALYSIS

CHAPTER Two presents the systematic seduction and abandonment of Marie, a domestic servant, by Franz, the same soldier from the previous chapter, during an evening at Vienna's Prater amusement park.

The narrative unfolds across two carefully structured scenes: the initial removal from the safety of Swoboda's dance hall into the dark park paths where Franz employs increasingly aggressive sexual pressure despite Marie's protests about the darkness and isolation; the sexual encounter itself in a secluded meadow followed by Franz's immediate emotional withdrawal and cruel dismissal of Marie's need for affection; and the return to the dance hall where Franz abandons Marie entirely to pursue a blonde woman, switching to refined High German speech that reveals his calculated social performance throughout the evening.

The plot demonstrates how predatory sexual behavior operates through environmental manipulation and false intimacy rather than direct coercion, with Franz systematically isolating Marie from witnesses and safety while creating an illusion of romantic interest that dissolves immediately after sexual gratification. Marie's journey from confident dancer to abandoned victim illustrates the particular vulnerability of "respectable" working-class women who lacked both the sexual experience of prostitutes and the economic protection of middle-class women, making them ideal targets for men seeking consequence-free sexual encounters.

Technical Structure and Literary Technique

Schnitzler employs masterful dramatic pacing that mirrors the psychological manipulation occurring within the narrative, using geographic movement from light to darkness and back to light as both literal plot development and symbolic representation of Marie's moral and emotional journey.

The author's dialogue-heavy technique reveals character psychology through speech patterns: Marie's increasingly fragmented protests ("But what are you doing... if I'd known this!") demonstrate her growing panic and internal conflict, while Franz's speech becomes more possessive and commanding as they move deeper into isolation, culminating in his blissful exclamation during the sexual encounter that reveals his complete self-absorption.

The scene structure functions as a compressed seduction narrative where each phase serves specific dramatic purposes: Scene One establishes the power dynamic and Franz's manipulative techniques; Scene Two exposes the brutal aftermath where emotional connection proves illusory; Scene Three demonstrates the cyclical nature of such exploitation as Franz immediately seeks new victims.

Schnitzler's use of environmental detail—the distant polka music, the darkness punctuated by cigarette glows, the contrast between the bright dance hall and the isolated meadow—creates atmospheric realism while reinforcing thematic elements about surface respectability concealing predatory behavior.

The author's strategic use of interruption and ellipsis during the seduction sequence allows readers to fill in details while maintaining the clinical detachment that characterizes his naturalistic style, preventing voyeuristic pleasure while forcing recognition of the encounter's exploitative nature.

Social Class Dynamics and Economic Vulnerability

The chapter provides devastating insight into how class privilege operates within the seemingly egalitarian space of public entertainment, where working-class people of different occupations might mingle socially yet remain trapped within rigid hierarchies that enable systematic exploitation.

Marie's position as a parlour maid places her in the precarious category of "respectable" working women who aspired to middle-class values while remaining economically vulnerable and socially isolated, making her particularly susceptible to manipulation by men who understood how to exploit her desire for genuine affection and social advancement.

Franz's behavior reveals how military status functioned as a form of class privilege that provided sexual access to civilian women across social boundaries, with his uniform serving as both attraction and implicit threat that complicated women's ability to refuse his advances safely.

The dance hall setting represents the new urban spaces where traditional chaperonage systems had broken down, creating opportunities for working-class women to socialize independently while simultaneously exposing them to predatory behavior from men who understood how to exploit these freedoms for sexual gratification. Marie's references to her mistress and fear of scolding reveal the additional layer of vulnerability faced by domestic servants whose employment depended entirely on maintaining reputations for moral propriety, making sexual exploitation not merely personally devastating but potentially economically ruinous.

Franz's immediate pursuit of the blonde woman after abandoning Marie demonstrates how such predatory patterns perpetuate across class lines, with working-class men like soldiers gaining access to multiple women through their symbolic authority while remaining economically unable to provide the security or commitment that might make such relationships genuinely reciprocal.

Gender Relations and Sexual Politics

The sexual encounter illuminates the profound gender asymmetries that structured male-female relationships across all social classes in late imperial Austria, where women's sexual agency was systematically constrained. At the same time, men enjoyed broad latitude for sexual experimentation without social consequences.

Marie's initial confidence in the dance hall—where she demonstrates social skills and exercises choice about partners—dissolves as Franz systematically removes her from spaces where she might receive protection or support, revealing how predatory men understand the geographic and social conditions necessary for sexual coercion. Her repeated concerns about darkness and isolation ("Look, it's so dark here. I'm getting frightened") demonstrate feminine intuition about danger that proves tragically accurate, while Franz's dismissive responses ("When I'm with you, you don't need to be afraid") employ protective rhetoric to mask predatory intentions.

The encounter's aftermath exposes the gendered nature of sexual shame and emotional labor in bourgeois society: while Franz experiences no psychological discomfort with his behavior and immediately seeks new conquests, Marie is left desperately seeking emotional validation ("At least tell me—do you care for me?") that might transform her exploitation into something approaching legitimate romantic experience.

Franz's linguistic code-switching when addressing the blonde woman—suddenly employing "cultured, proper High German"—reveals the calculated nature of his earlier performance with Marie, demonstrating how predatory men adapt their presentation to exploit different women's particular vulnerabilities and desires. Marie's jealousy about the blonde woman with the "ugly face" reflects internalized feminine competition that prevents solidarity between women who share similar vulnerabilities, while Franz's casual dismissal of her concerns reveals masculine indifference to the emotional consequences of sexual exploitation.

Historical Context and Cultural Commentary

For contemporary readers, several elements require historical contextualization to fully appreciate Schnitzler's social critique of fin-de-siècle Viennese society.

The Prater represents Vienna's primary public recreation space, where different social classes mingled in ways that would have been impossible in more formal social settings, with the Wurstelprater amusement area providing a carnival atmosphere that temporarily suspended normal social conventions while creating opportunities for sexual encounters across class boundaries.

Swoboda's dance hall exemplifies the "penny dance" culture that allowed working-class people to socialize for minimal cost, with the polka music representing popular entertainment that brought together soldiers, domestic servants, and other working people in spaces relatively free from bourgeois supervision.

Franz's midnight barracks curfew reflects the rigid discipline of Habsburg military life, where soldiers faced severe punishment for tardiness, making his time pressure genuine rather than merely an excuse for rushing the sexual encounter, though his willingness to risk punishment for dancing rather than accompanying Marie home reveals his priorities clearly.

Marie's employment as a parlour maid indicates her position within the hierarchy of domestic service, where she would have been responsible for maintaining reception rooms and serving guests, requiring literacy, social skills, and personal presentation that distinguished her from general housekeepers or scullery maids while leaving her equally vulnerable to sexual exploitation by employers or their social contacts.

Psychological Realism and Thematic Significance

Schnitzler's psychological penetration reveals how sexual exploitation operates through sophisticated emotional manipulation rather than simple physical coercion, with Franz demonstrating an intuitive understanding of Marie's particular vulnerabilities as a woman seeking genuine affection and social validation within the limited opportunities available to working-class people.

His technique of creating false intimacy through personal compliments, protective gestures, and requests for informal address demonstrates predatory sophistication that exploits feminine socialization patterns that encourage women to interpret male attention as evidence of romantic interest rather than sexual opportunism.

Marie's psychological journey from confidence to vulnerability to desperate hope illustrates how women internalize responsibility for sexual encounters even when they result from systematic manipulation, with her final plea for emotional validation representing tragic attempts to preserve dignity within fundamentally degrading circumstances.

The encounter's failure to provide satisfaction for either participant—Franz gains physical gratification but no genuine connection, while Marie receives neither emotional fulfillment nor social advancement—exemplifies Schnitzler's central critique of how modern urban life transforms intimate human experiences into mechanical exchanges that leave all parties emotionally impoverished.

The chapter's integration into the larger "round dance" structure becomes apparent through Franz's serial pursuit of different women and Marie's earlier correspondence with other men, suggesting that such patterns of brief connection and abandonment represent recurring cycles rather than isolated incidents, creating networks of sexual exploitation that perpetuate social alienation while maintaining facades of romantic interaction.

Franz's immediate return to predatory behavior after abandoning Marie demonstrates how such exploitation becomes habituated masculine behavior that operates independently of individual women's particular qualities or circumstances, while Marie's isolation at the chapter's conclusion illustrates how sexual exploitation functions to atomize working-class women and prevent the solidarity that might challenge such systematic abuse.

The chapter ultimately functions as a devastating critique of how class and gender privilege intersect to enable sexual colonization of vulnerable women within the apparently civilized context of urban entertainment culture, revealing how spaces of apparent freedom and social mixing actually facilitate systematic exploitation while maintaining ideological frameworks that blame individual women for their victimization rather than challenging the social structures that enable predatory masculine behavior.

CHAPTER 3: "THE PARLOUR MAID AND THE YOUNG GENTLEMAN"

SUMMARY AND PLOT ANALYSIS

CHAPTER Three depicts the methodical seduction of Marie, a parlour maid, by Alfred, the young son of the wealthy household where she works. The action unfolds on a hot summer afternoon when the family has departed for their country estate, leaving the house nearly empty.

Through a series of increasingly transparent pretexts—requests for cognac, water, and medical information—Alfred lures Marie into his room where he systematically breaks down her resistance through a combination of physical attraction, flattery, and implicit threats to her employment.

The encounter begins with seemingly innocent requests for service but escalates through intimate compliments about her clothing and skin to sexual contact, interrupted by an unwelcome visitor who causes Alfred's immediate post-coital shame and cruel dismissal of Marie.

The chapter concludes with Alfred's cold departure to the coffeehouse and Marie's small act of defiance in stealing one of his cigars, suggesting both her residual dignity and the transactional nature of their encounter.

Technical Structure and Dramatic Technique

Schnitzler constructs this chapter as a masterpiece of psychological manipulation rendered through dramatic technique, employing what might be called "seduction by degrees" where each seemingly innocent request increases the intimacy between master and servant.

The three-scene structure mirrors classical dramatic progression: the initial "innocent" encounters where Alfred tests boundaries through service requests, the central seduction scene where power dynamics become explicit, and the aftermath where social hierarchy brutally reasserts itself.

The author creates an almost voyeuristic experience for readers who observe the manipulation unfold in real time. The sparse descriptive passages function like theatrical lighting, with the lowered blinds creating an atmosphere of secrecy and transgression that literally dims the moral clarity of the situation.

Schnitzler's technique of interruption—the mysterious bell that rings at the crucial moment—serves both as dramatic device and social commentary, suggesting that even in moments of apparent privacy, the broader social world intrudes to remind characters of their proper roles.

Social Class Dynamics and Power Relations

The chapter operates as a devastating critique of how class privilege enables sexual exploitation within the apparently civilized confines of bourgeois domesticity. Alfred's behavior demonstrates the particular vulnerability of domestic servants who, unlike prostitutes or working women in public spaces, cannot escape their exploiters and remain economically dependent on their abusers' discretion and good will.

Marie occupies a precarious position as a "respectable" working woman whose employment depends entirely on maintaining her reputation, yet whose isolation in the household makes her an easy target for her employer's son. The power imbalance is absolute: Alfred can destroy Marie's livelihood with a word to his parents, making her resistance not merely difficult but economically suicidal. His casual assumption of sexual access to household staff reflects aristocratic attitudes toward servant sexuality that treated working-class women's bodies as extensions of their labor—available for any purpose their betters deemed appropriate.

Historical Context and Social Commentary

For modern readers, several elements require historical context to fully appreciate Schnitzler's social critique.

The "estate" refers to the grand urban residences of wealthy Viennese families who maintained both city houses and country properties, retreating to the countryside during hot summers and leaving skeleton staff to maintain their urban establishments.

The parlour maid held a relatively privileged position among domestic servants, responsible for maintaining the family's reception rooms and serving guests, requiring more refinement and education than scullery maids or general housekeepers. Her ability to read and write, evidenced by her letter to Franz the soldier, marks her as part of the "respectable" working class that aspired to middle-class values while remaining economically vulnerable.

The locked cognac cabinet reflects not only the value of imported spirits but also the masters' distrust of their servants, while Alfred's casual mention of reading French novels signals both his educated leisure and the period's association of French literature with moral corruption.

The coffeehouse culture central to Viennese social life functioned as an extension of male domestic space where gentlemen could conduct business, read newspapers, and socialize away from family supervision, making Alfred's retreat there after his sexual encounter both socially acceptable and morally cowardly.

Interpersonal Psychology and Gender Dynamics

The psychological complexity of the encounter reveals how sexual exploitation operates through emotional manipulation rather than simple physical force.

Alfred's technique demonstrates sophisticated understanding of his victim's psychology: he begins with legitimate service requests that establish his authority, progresses to personal compliments that create false intimacy, and culminates in physical contact that he presents as natural appreciation rather than sexual aggression.

His repeated observations about Marie's appearance—her blue blouse, white skin, pleasant-smelling hair—function as both seductive flattery and possessive cataloguing, treating her body as an object for aesthetic appreciation rather than recognizing her as a complete human being.

Marie's responses reveal the tragic bind of working-class women who must choose between economic survival and personal dignity: her protests become increasingly feeble as she recognizes the futility of resistance, while her attempt to maintain conversational normalcy ("The young master flatters me") shows her desperate effort to preserve some shred of respectability even as it dissolves.

The encounter's aftermath brutally exposes the gendered nature of sexual shame in bourgeois society: while Alfred experiences immediate disgust and rejection of intimacy, seeking to restore social distance through his harsh dismissal and retreat to male social spaces, Marie is left with both physical vulnerability and emotional abandonment, her theft of the cigar representing a pathetic attempt to claim some small compensation for her exploitation.

Literary Technique and Thematic Significance

Schnitzler's clinical presentation style, influenced by his medical background, creates analytical distance that prevents readers from becoming emotionally invested in the characters while forcing recognition of the social mechanisms that enable exploitation.

The author's use of repetitive dialogue patterns—Alfred's multiple summons, Marie's increasingly nervous responses—creates a hypnotic quality that mirrors the psychological manipulation occurring within the narrative.

The chapter's integration into the larger "round dance" structure becomes apparent through Marie's earlier letter to Franz the soldier, suggesting that she has already been sexually compromised and is now passing through another stage of the endless cycle of exploitation that defines working-class women's relationships with men of all social levels.

The symbolic significance of the locked cognac cabinet and Marie's final theft of the cigar reveals how the domestic sphere operates as a site of both material and sexual appropriation, where wealthy families control access to luxury items just as they control access to their servants' bodies.

Alfred's immediate shame and rejection following the sexual encounter exposes the fundamental hypocrisy of bourgeois morality that creates desire for transgression while demanding the preservation of social proprieties, leaving working-class women to bear the consequences of their employers' moral contradictions.

The chapter ultimately functions as a devastating indictment of how class privilege operates in the most intimate spaces, revealing the domestic sphere as a site of sexual colonization where the rhetoric of protection and care masks relationships of exploitation and abandonment that leave working-class women emotionally and economically devastated while allowing privileged men to return to their social worlds without consequence or accountability.

CHAPTER 4: "THE YOUNG GENTLEMAN AND THE YOUNG WIFE"

Summary and Plot Analysis

CHAPTER FOUR PRESENTS THE elaborate seduction of Emma, a married bourgeois woman, by Alfred, the wealthy young gentleman from the last chapter, in his carefully prepared apartment on Vienna's Schwindgasse.

The narrative unfolds across four meticulously structured scenes that trace the complete arc from anticipation through consummation to aftermath and departure.

The opening scene reveals Alfred's theatrical preparations—perfuming the rooms with violet spray, arranging cognac and delicacies, hiding evidence of previous liaisons—before Emma's heavily veiled arrival for what she insists will be only a "five-minute" visit.

The subsequent scenes chronicle Alfred's systematic dismantling of Emma's resistance through flattery, physical comfort, and emotional manipulation, culminating in their movement to the bedroom where the sexual encounter occurs.

The aftermath proves particularly revealing as Alfred experiences immediate performance anxiety and intellectual pretension, citing Stendhal's "Psychology of Love" to rationalize his sexual inadequacy while Emma attempts to maintain dignity through humor and maternal comfort.

The final scene depicts Emma's anxious departure as she faces the practical consequences of her adultery—explaining her absence to her sister—while Alfred's concluding thought reveals his smug satisfaction at having conquered "a respectable woman," demonstrating how the encounter serves different psychological needs for each participant.

Technical Structure and Literary Technique

Schnitzler employs a sophisticated four-act structure that mirrors classical dramatic progression while incorporating naturalistic attention to psychological detail and social environment.

The opening scene functions as elaborate exposition, revealing Alfred's calculated preparation and bourgeois pretensions through his careful arrangement of luxury items—the silver tray with cognac, glazed chestnuts, violet perfume—that create an atmosphere of refined seduction designed to appeal to middle-class feminine sensibilities.

Schnitzler's dialogue technique reveals character psychology through speech patterns: Emma's nervous repetition of time concerns and moral protestations demonstrate her internal conflict between desire and social obligation, while Alfred's alternation between wounded romanticism and intellectual pretension exposes his fundamental immaturity and self-absorption.

The bedroom scene employs strategic ellipsis and fragmented dialogue to convey sexual tension while maintaining the analytical detachment characteristic of naturalistic literature, refusing to romanticize the encounter while documenting its psychological complexities.

The author's use of temporal specificity—the precise timing of Emma's arrival at "quarter past seven" and departure at "eight o'clock"—creates dramatic tension while emphasizing how adultery must be carefully scheduled around bourgeois domestic obligations, transforming passion into another form of social appointment that must be managed within existing structures of respectability.

Social Class Dynamics and Bourgeois Culture

The chapter provides devastating insight into how bourgeois marriage and sexual morality operate to constrain authentic human connection while creating opportunities for systematic hypocrisy and exploitation.

Alfred's apartment on Schwindgasse represents the emerging culture of urban bachelor establishments where wealthy young men could conduct affairs away from family supervision, with the "banal elegance" of the furnishings reflecting nouveau riche pretensions that prioritize expensive display over genuine aesthetic sophistication.

Emma's position as a married woman from the respectable bourgeoisie makes her both more desirable as a conquest and more vulnerable to social destruction if discovered, creating the particular tension that drives upper-class adultery where the stakes involve not merely personal shame but complete social ostracism and economic ruin.

Alfred's casual mention of having attended the Industrialists' Ball with Emma and her husband reveals how Vienna's bourgeois social calendar created opportunities for adultery within the very institutions designed to reinforce marriage and family stability, with formal social occasions providing cover for the cultivation of illicit relationships.

The economic dimensions of their affair become apparent through Emma's anxiety about explaining her absence and Alfred's confidence that their social circles will provide future opportunities for contact, demonstrating how class privilege creates networks of discretion and complicity that enable systematic marital infidelity while maintaining public facades of moral propriety.

Emma's husband, mentioned casually throughout their encounter, represents the absent bourgeois patriarch whose economic provision and social status create the very conditions of leisure and luxury that enable his wife's adultery, illustrating how bourgeois marriage transforms women into consumers of experiences rather than equal partners in genuine intimate relationships.

Gender Relations and Sexual Politics

The sexual encounter reveals the profound contradictions within bourgeois gender ideology that simultaneously elevated women as moral guardians while denying them agency over their own desires and sexuality.

Emma's heavily veiled arrival and repeated insistence on the brief duration of her visit demonstrate how respectable women internalized shame about sexual desire while seeking ways to experience passion within socially acceptable frameworks of romantic love and emotional connection.

Alfred's seduction technique relies heavily on creating false intimacy through personal compliments, protective gestures, and romantic rhetoric that transforms sexual desire into seemingly elevated emotional experience, appealing to feminine socialization that encouraged women to interpret male attention as evidence of genuine affection rather than sexual opportunism.

The power dynamics shift throughout their encounter: Emma initially maintains control through her time restrictions and moral protestations, but Alfred gradually assumes dominance through environmental manipulation—controlling lighting, refreshments, and physical comfort—that creates psychological conditions favorable to seduction.

The sexual encounter itself, notably elliptical in Schnitzler's presentation, is followed immediately by Alfred's performance anxiety and intellectual defensiveness, revealing how bourgeois masculine identity depended on sexual competence that actual experience often failed to provide, leading to compensatory displays of cultural sophistication and emotional manipulation.

Emma's maternal response to Alfred's sexual inadequacy—comforting him and making light of his embarrassment—demonstrates how women were expected to manage masculine emotional fragility even in contexts where they were being sexually exploited, while her own needs for emotional validation remain largely unacknowledged throughout their encounter.

Historical Context and Cultural Commentary

For contemporary readers, several elements require historical contextualization to appreciate fully Schnitzler's critique of fin-de-siècle Viennese bourgeois culture.

Schwindgasse, located in Vienna's fourth district, represents the type of respectable middle-class neighborhood where bachelor apartments and discrete furnished rooms provided venues for extramarital affairs, with the ironic street name ("Swindle Street") adding literary commentary on the deceptive nature of such arrangements.

The elaborate preparations Alfred makes—violet perfume, cognac, glazed chestnuts—reflect the consumer culture emerging in late imperial Vienna where luxury goods became associated with sophisticated sexuality and romantic refinement, contrasting sharply with the more directly transactional encounters between working-class characters in earlier chapters.

Emma's multiple veils and concern about recognition on the stairs illustrate the elaborate precautions required for bourgeois adultery, where social reputation represented the primary form of wealth for married women and discovery could result in complete social and economic destruction.

The references to formal social events like the Industrialists' Ball and the Lobheimers' upcoming gathering reveal how Vienna's bourgeois social calendar created structured opportunities for cultivating illicit relationships within apparently respectable contexts, with the formal protocols of balls and dinner parties providing cover for intimate conversations and romantic development.

Alfred's citation of Stendhal's "Psychology of Love" reflects the period's intellectual culture, where French literature and philosophy provided sophisticated frameworks for discussing sexuality and emotion, allowing educated men to rationalize sexual behavior through reference to literary authority while maintaining pretenses of cultural refinement.

Psychological Realism and Performance of Intimacy

Schnitzler's psychological penetration reveals how bourgeois sexual relationships become performances of romantic intimacy that serve individual psychological needs rather than creating genuine human connection between equal partners.

Alfred's elaborate preparations and theatrical staging of the seduction demonstrate how bourgeois masculinity required constant performance of cultural sophistication and romantic sensitivity to distinguish upper-class sexual behavior from working-class directness, with the apartment's "banal elegance" reflecting his fundamental insecurity about his own cultural authenticity.

Emma's internal conflict between sexual desire and moral obligation illustrates how bourgeois feminine identity depended on maintaining simultaneous claims to moral purity and emotional sensitivity, creating psychological contradictions that made authentic self-expression nearly impossible within existing social frameworks.

The encounter's aftermath, where Alfred immediately intellectualizes his sexual performance through reference to literary authority while Emma focuses on practical concerns about maintaining her domestic deceptions, reveals how different gender socialization creates fundamentally incompatible approaches to sexual experience and emotional intimacy.

Alfred's concluding satisfaction at having "an affair with a respectable woman" exposes how bourgeois adultery functions primarily as social achievement rather than genuine romantic connection, with Emma's married status representing a conquest that confirms his masculine sophistication rather than evidence of mutual attraction or emotional compatibility.

Thematic Significance and Social Critique

The chapter serves as a devastating critique of how bourgeois social structures corrupt authentic human relationships by transforming them into performances of class status and gender conformity that leave all participants emotionally unsatisfied while maintaining facades of romantic fulfillment and cultural sophistication.

The "round dance" metaphor becomes particularly evident as Emma moves from her marriage to Alfred while he simultaneously positions himself for future conquests, creating chains of connection and abandonment that perpetuate social atomization rather than genuine community or lasting intimacy. Schnitzler's clinical presentation refuses to romanticize the affair while documenting its psychological costs:

Emma faces genuine danger to her social and economic security, while Alfred gains only temporary ego gratification that requires constant renewal through new conquests.

The chapter's integration into the larger cycle structure reveals how bourgeois sexual relationships operate according to the same mechanical patterns as working-class encounters, despite their elaborate cultural packaging and pretensions to elevated emotional content.

The author's medical background becomes apparent in his unflinching analysis of how social structures shape individual psychology, with both characters remaining trapped within predetermined roles that prevent authentic self-expression or mutual recognition.

Emma's final departure into the anxiety of domestic deception while Alfred retreats into smug self-congratulation illustrates how bourgeois adultery ultimately serves to reinforce rather than challenge existing social hierarchies, providing safety valves for individual frustration while maintaining the fundamental structures of marriage, class privilege, and gender inequality that create the need for such escape mechanisms in the first place.

CHAPTER 5: "THE YOUNG WIFE AND THE HUSBAND"

Summary and Plot Analysis

CHAPTER FIVE PRESENTS AN intimate bedroom conversation between Emma, the young wife from the previous chapter, and her husband Karl, occurring the same evening after her return from her affair with Alfred.

The narrative unfolds across three carefully structured scenes that reveal the psychological aftermath of adultery within the context of bourgeois marriage.

The opening scene depicts Karl entering their bedroom at half past ten, finding Emma reading in bed, and initiating what becomes an extended philosophical discussion about the nature of marriage, love, and sexual morality. Karl expounds his theory that successful marriages require alternating periods of friendship and passion, claiming that constant romantic intensity would destroy the "sanctity" of marriage.

The conversation takes a provocative turn when Emma begins questioning Karl about his past sexual experiences, particularly whether he has ever been involved with a married woman, creating dramatic irony as she herself has just committed adultery.

The subsequent intimate scene reveals Emma's internal conflict as she lies beside her sleeping husband, tormented by memories of her afternoon with Alfred while contemplating the dangerous double life she has begun.

Karl's Character and Bourgeois Philosophy

Karl embodies the intellectual pretensions and moral contradictions of the educated bourgeois patriarch who attempts to rationalize sexual behavior through philosophical frameworks that preserve masculine privilege while constraining feminine agency.

His elaborate theory about marriage requiring alternating periods of passion and friendship reveals how bourgeois men intellectualized their sexual relationships to maintain control over their wives' expectations and emotional needs, creating pseudo-scientific justifications for withholding consistent affection and intimacy.

Karl's condescending tone when discussing women's sexual ignorance—referring to Emma as "my child" and explaining how men become "confused and uncertain" through their pre-marital experiences while women remain "pure and ignorant"—demonstrates the paternalistic attitudes that reduced wives to children requiring masculine guidance and protection from dangerous knowledge about sexuality and the world.

Karl's discussion of prostitutes reveals the fundamental hypocrisy of bourgeois sexual morality that enabled men to exploit working-class women while maintaining moral superiority through expressions of pity and concern for their "misery." His claim that such women are "destined by nature to fall deeper and deeper" reflects social Darwinist ideas about moral degeneracy that allowed middle-class men to rationalize their participation in systems of sexual exploitation while preserving their self-image as morally superior beings who understood the tragic necessities of masculine sexual development.

The revelation about his past affair with a married woman "who is dead" adds melodramatic weight to his moral warnings while demonstrating how bourgeois men constructed tragic narratives around their sexual histories that positioned them as victims of feminine manipulation rather than active participants in adultery.

Emma's Psychological Complexity

Emma emerges as a far more psychologically complex character than her husband, caught between genuine curiosity about sexuality and relationships, growing awareness of her own capacity for transgression, and desperate attempts to maintain her role as the ideal bourgeois wife.

Her persistent questioning about Karl's past experiences reveals both intellectual curiosity and a growing understanding of the sexual double standards that govern her marriage, while her playful suggestion that she would like to be his "mistress a little" demonstrates growing awareness of the different types of relationships possible between men and women beyond the pure wife role.

The dramatic irony of her questions about married women among Karl's past lovers becomes particularly poignant given her recent affair with Alfred, suggesting both genuine curiosity about whether other women in her position have transgressed and perhaps a subconscious desire for confession or absolution.

Marital Dynamics and Sexual Politics

The bedroom conversation reveals how bourgeois marriage functioned as an institution that managed and controlled female sexuality while providing men with regular access to sexual gratification without the risks or complications associated with extramarital affairs.

Karl's philosophy about alternating friendship and passion periods serves to justify his emotional withholding while maintaining Emma's sexual availability, creating a system where masculine needs for variety and autonomy are preserved while feminine needs for consistent affection and emotional security remain unmet. The power dynamics of their conversation become apparent through Karl's patronizing explanations and Emma's careful navigation between genuine curiosity and dangerous territory that might reveal her own transgressive thoughts or experiences.

The sexual encounter that follows their philosophical discussion demonstrates how bourgeois marital intimacy operates according to masculine schedules and priorities, with Karl initiating contact when he feels "lonely" at his desk rather than responding to Emma's emotional or physical needs. Emma's comparison of their lovemaking to their Venice honeymoon suggests both nostalgia for early romantic passion and recognition that their current relationship lacks the intensity and spontaneity that once characterized their connection.

Historical Context and Social Commentary

The late bedtime hour of "half past ten" reflects the leisurely lifestyle of the bourgeoisie who could afford gas lighting and domestic servants, while Karl's reference to working at his desk suggests the professional or business activities that provided middle-class families with economic security but required men to spend long hours away from domestic life.

Emma's reading in bed demonstrates the literacy and leisure time available to bourgeois women, though her access to books would have been carefully monitored to prevent exposure to morally dangerous literature that might encourage inappropriate thoughts or desires.

The Venice honeymoon reference evokes the grand tour tradition where wealthy couples traveled to romantic destinations for extended wedding trips, with Venice representing the height of romantic and cultural sophistication for Austrian tourists.

Karl's discussion of prostitutes and "fallen women" reflects contemporary debates about sexual morality and social reform that characterized progressive intellectual circles in Vienna, where medical and psychological theories about sexuality were beginning to challenge traditional religious approaches to sexual behavior.

The mention of "young girls from good families" refers to the standard bourgeois marriage pattern where virginal women from respectable backgrounds married experienced men who were expected to provide sexual guidance and education within the safety of legal matrimony.

Thematic Significance and Literary Technique

Schnitzler employs dramatic irony masterfully throughout the chapter, as readers understand the full significance of Emma's questions about adultery and her internal conflicts while Karl remains completely unaware of his wife's recent transgression, creating tension that transforms their seemingly innocent conversation into a psychological minefield where every exchange carries multiple layers of meaning.

The author documents the psychological costs of sexual repression and the double standards that govern bourgeois marriage, with both characters trapped within social roles that prevent authentic communication or emotional intimacy despite their physical proximity and legal union.

The chapter's integration into the larger "round dance" structure becomes evident through Emma's movement between different sexual partners while maintaining her primary identity as Karl's wife, suggesting that bourgeois adultery operates according to the same cyclical patterns as working-class sexual encounters despite the elaborate moral and philosophical frameworks used to justify or condemn such behavior.

Emma's final embrace of her identity as "a woman with a lover" represents a psychological transformation that positions her outside the boundaries of respectable feminine identity while remaining physically and legally trapped within her marriage, creating the fundamental tension that will drive her future actions and choices.

CHAPTER 6: "THE HUSBAND AND THE SWEET GIRL"

Summary and Plot Analysis

CHAPTER SIX PRESENTS KARL'S affair with an unnamed nineteen-year-old working-class girl in a private dining room at the Riedhof restaurant.

The narrative unfolds across three scenes that chronicle a complete seduction from intimate dinner through sexual encounter to Karl's calculated plans for future meetings.

The opening scene depicts their after-dinner conversation as the girl savors cream pastries while Karl smokes his Havana cigar, establishing the power dynamic between the wealthy married man and the economically vulnerable young woman. Their conversation reveals her family circumstances—living with her mother and four siblings, working as a domestic helper while her sister Kathi works in a flower shop, and her brother studies to become a teacher.

The sexual encounter occurs gradually as Karl manipulates the girl's obvious attraction to him and her intoxication from Hungarian white wine, leading to their movement to the divan, where he systematically breaks down her resistance.

Karl's Manipulative Technique

Karl demonstrates sophisticated predatory behavior that exploits class differences and the girl's inexperience with wealthy men who possess cultural capital and social confidence. His questioning about her previous lovers reveals both jealousy and the need to categorize her sexual experience, alternating between assumptions about her promiscuity and satisfaction when she claims innocence. Karl's estimate of "twenty" previous lovers exposes his contempt for working-class women's morality while his pleasure at her protestations reveals his desire to believe himself special in her affections.

Karl's casual claim about living in Graz rather than Vienna demonstrates how married men maintained affairs by claiming to live in another city, creating geographic distance that prevented emotional entanglement while providing excuses for irregular contact.

His angry reaction when the girl suggests his wife "doesn't act any differently" reveals the profound double standard that allowed bourgeois men sexual freedom while demanding absolute fidelity from their wives. The prohibition against discussing his wife exposes how such affairs depend on maintaining strict psychological compartmentalization between domestic responsibilities and sexual adventures.

The Sweet Girl's Vulnerability

The unnamed girl embodies the "süßes Mädel" archetype—young working-class women who occupied a precarious position between respectability and sexual availability in fin-de-siècle Vienna. Her family circumstances reveal the economic pressures that made such relationships attractive: supporting four siblings while working as a domestic helper, with dreams of respectability through her brother's education and her sister's flower shop employment.

Her obvious inexperience with fine dining and wine creates dramatic contrast with Karl's sophistication, while her pleasure in simple luxuries like cream pastries emphasizes the material temptations such relationships offered to working-class women.

Her repeated insistence that "there must have been something in that wine" reveals both genuine confusion about her own desires and desperate need to maintain some claim to moral innocence despite her obvious attraction to Karl.

The girl's confession about her previous lover who "looked a little like" Karl suggests both vulnerability to masculine types and possible psychological manipulation of older men through appeal to their vanity.

Her family responsibilities—watching her younger sister's moral behavior and managing household affairs—demonstrate how working-class women bore disproportionate responsibility for family reputation and survival.

Social and Economic Dynamics

The private dining room at the Riedhof restaurant represents the bourgeois infrastructure that enabled discreet extramarital affairs, with expensive meals and wine creating an atmosphere of sophistication that distinguished such encounters from direct prostitution while serving identical functions.

ARTHUR SCHNITZLER

Karl's ability to afford Hungarian white wine, Havana cigars, and private dining demonstrates how economic privilege provided access to working-class women who could be impressed by displays of wealth and cultural refinement.

The girl's anxiety about explaining her late return home reveals how such relationships required working-class women to risk their family relationships and reputations for temporary access to bourgeois luxury.

The conversation about theater attendance through her brother's barbering connections illuminates how working-class families created networks of mutual support and occasional access to cultural experiences normally beyond their economic reach.

Her brother's aspiration to become a teacher represents working-class hopes for social mobility through education, while her role managing household discipline shows how family survival depended on careful moral management and mutual surveillance.

Psychological Manipulation and Class Exploitation

Karl's seduction technique relies heavily on creating false intimacy through personal interest in her family circumstances and apparent respect for her domestic responsibilities, appealing to working-class values about family loyalty and moral propriety while systematically undermining her resistance to sexual advances.

His comments about her resembling "someone from my youth" reveal how bourgeois men nostalgically romanticized working-class femininity while exploiting actual working-class women for sexual gratification. The girl's comparison of Karl to her previous lover suggests how such relationships perpetuate cycles where working-class women become psychologically vulnerable to men who exploit their emotional needs and economic circumstances.

The encounter's conclusion, where Karl arranges future meetings while maintaining clear boundaries about his availability and expectations, demonstrates how bourgeois men structured extramarital affairs to maximize their pleasure while minimizing their obligations or emotional investment. His insistence on her exclusive fidelity while maintaining his own marriage reveals the fundamental inequality that characterized such relationships, where working-class women provided sexual and emotional services while receiving minimal security or genuine affection in return.

CHAPTER 7: "THE SWEET GIRL AND THE POET"

CHAPTER 7 PRESENTS AN intimate encounter between a poet and a young woman known simply as "the sweet girl" in his private apartment. The poet, who claims to write under the pseudonym "Biebitz," strategically seduces the young woman through romantic pretensions and manipulation of the dimly lit environment.

The setting itself—a tastefully furnished room with a writing desk, scattered books, and a piano—establishes the poet's cultural capital and bohemian persona. His deliberate maintenance of darkness ("twilight like a bathrobe") creates both intimacy and a power imbalance, as he can see her while she cannot fully see him.

Throughout their interaction, the poet employs literary devices and metaphors ("castle in India") to romanticize their encounter, even pausing to record phrases in his notebook that he might use in his work. This reveals his commodification of the experience—she is not only a sexual conquest but also source material.

The class distinction between them is evident in their dialogue. The sweet girl's confusion about his profession ("I thought writers are all doctors") reveals her limited education and social position. The poet, meanwhile, fetishizes her supposed simplicity, calling it "divine" and "sacred," reflecting the period's romanticization of working-class women as more "natural" and uncorrupted by modern sophistication.

Social constraints of 1890s Vienna are apparent in the sweet girl's concerns about being seen together ("if mother hears something") and her obligation to family responsibilities. Women of her class faced strict moral supervision, with reputation being their primary social currency.

The sexual politics are particularly revealing. The poet's seduction techniques—from insisting she remove her clothing while he remains dressed to promising future theater tickets—establish an uneven exchange. His talk of a temporary countryside idyll ending in a clean break ("one day farewell") suggests he views her as a temporary diversion rather than a serious relationship prospect.

For modern readers, terms like "chambre separée" (private dining rooms in restaurants used for romantic trysts), "mantilla" (a lace veil worn over the head), and "bodice" (a structured upper garment) provide important cultural context for understanding the coded language of intimacy in this era. Similarly, the reference to "Cavalleria" (a popular opera) and the Burgtheater (Vienna's prestigious imperial theater) establishes the cultural touchstones that separated their worlds.

By the scene's end, the poet has already scheduled their next meeting around a performance of his supposed friend Biebitz's play—continuing the web of half-truths that characterize his approach to the relationship and setting up what will likely be further exploitation under the guise of romance.

CHAPTER 8: "THE POET AND THE ACTRESS"

CHAPTER 8 SHIFTS DRAMATICALLY in setting and class dynamics, moving from urban Vienna to a rural country inn where the Poet and Actress conduct their romantic liaison. The moonlit countryside setting creates an atmosphere of theatrical romance that mirrors the Actress's professional world.

The Actress immediately establishes her dominance through a performance of religious devotion, kneeling in prayer by the window in a calculated display that combines spirituality with seduction. Her sudden turn to prayer reflects the complex relationship between sexuality and Catholic devotion in Austrian society, where theatrical personalities often maintained religious practices alongside unconventional lifestyles.

The Poet's bewilderment at her prayer reveals his intellectual skepticism about religion, typical of literary circles that viewed faith as incompatible with artistic sophistication. The Actress's sharp retort that she's "no pale scoundrel" suggests that atheism was associated with moral corruption, particularly among bohemian intellectuals.

The revelation that she was "praying to you" transforms religious worship into romantic idolatry, demonstrating the Actress's ability to theatricalize every gesture and blur sacred and profane love. This manipulation of religious imagery shows her sophisticated understanding of dramatic effect, even in private moments.

The location's history emerges when the Actress reveals she previously stayed here "for years" with Fritz, her former lover. This transforms their romantic getaway into a recycled setting, suggesting both practical familiarity and emotional baggage that undermines the Poet's assumptions about their unique connection.

The Actress's dismissal of the Poet's literary pretensions ("if you happened to have talent") reveals the competitive cruelty between artistic personalities, each seeking to establish superiority over the other. Her cutting remarks contrast sharply with the sweet submission the Poet experienced with the previous young woman.

The Poet's flowery compliments ("you are a world unto yourself... sacred simplicity") echo his earlier seduction techniques, revealing his formulaic approach to romantic conquest. His repetition of the "sacred simplicity" phrase from the previous chapter exposes his limited vocabulary of romantic idealization.

The Actress's practical control over their encounter emerges through her management of privacy, lighting, and timing. She dismisses him while she undresses, then summons him back, maintaining authority over the physical and emotional rhythm of their liaison.

Their post-coital conversation reveals the Actress's theatrical personality extending into intimate moments. Her claim of "forty degrees" fever from longing for him employs medical imagery for dramatic effect, while her rapid emotional shifts between passion and dismissal demonstrate her performer's instinct for keeping audiences off-balance.

The dispute over night sounds—whether crickets or frogs—becomes a microcosm of their broader conflict between the Poet's romantic literariness and the Actress's practical directness. His insistence on crickets reflects his need to poeticize every experience, while her correction to frogs asserts empirical reality over romantic fantasy.

The reference to Benno having "an affair with his postman" provides insight into how homosexuality was discussed in coded language during this period of legal prohibition.

The Actress's revelation that she's betraying someone while refusing to specify whom creates another layer of theatrical mystery. Her performance anxiety about the Poet's absence from the theater reveals how professional and personal validation intertwine for performing artists.

The chapter concludes with the Actress's dismissal of Fritz as a "galley slave," demonstrating her ability to rewrite emotional history to suit present circumstances while maintaining her pattern of intense romantic attachments followed by complete rejection.

CHAPTER 9: "THE ACTRESS AND THE COUNT"

CHAPTER 9 PRESENTS THE culmination of Schnitzler's social hierarchy, bringing together Vienna's theatrical elite and military aristocracy in an opulent bedroom setting that reflects the Actress's financial success and social aspirations. The noon setting with drawn blinds establishes the bohemian lifestyle of theatrical performers who worked evenings and maintained inverted daily schedules.

The Count's entrance in dragoon cavalry uniform immediately establishes his elite military status, as dragoons were prestigious mounted units typically reserved for aristocratic officers. His formal request for permission from the Actress's mother reveals adherence to social proprieties even in what becomes an intimate encounter, demonstrating how aristocratic codes of conduct persisted even in transgressive situations.

The Actress's performance of illness ("I was near death!") transforms her bedroom into a stage where she can manipulate the Count's sympathy while maintaining theatrical grandeur. Her selective placement of only his flowers in her private space, while leaving others in the dressing room, demonstrates sophisticated romantic strategy that flatters his ego while suggesting special favor.

The Count's philosophical musings about happiness, pleasure, and the meaninglessness of conventional romantic categories reflect aristocratic ennui and intellectual sophistication. His dismissal of love as non-existent while acknowledging "pleasure" and "intoxication" as real reveals a worldview shaped by privilege and emotional detachment that protects him from genuine vulnerability.

The Actress's aggressive pursuit challenges traditional gender roles, as she takes the sexual initiative while the Count retreats into abstract philosophizing. Her direct physical advances and demand for immediate gratification contrast sharply with his preference for elaborate evening rituals involving carriages, supper, and gradual romantic progression.

The Count's resistance to morning intimacy ("I find love horrible" before breakfast) reflects aristocratic notions about appropriate timing for various activities, where proper romance required evening settings, formal dining, and elaborate social choreography. His insistence on "mood" reveals class-based assumptions about how romantic encounters should unfold.

The Actress's mockery of his refinement ("you old man," "poseur," "wretched poseur") attacks his masculine pride while exposing the performative nature of aristocratic sexual conduct. Her theatrical training gives her tools to manipulate and wound that match his social advantages, creating a battle between different forms of cultural capital.

The Count's comparison to "Miss Birken" reveals the network of relationships between aristocratic men and theatrical women, suggesting that such affairs followed recognizable patterns. His casual mention of this other liaison demonstrates the commodified nature of these relationships from the male aristocratic perspective.

The sexual encounter occurs despite the Count's philosophical resistance, as the Actress's immediate physical demands override his preference for delayed gratification. Her transformation of afternoon into metaphorical "evening" and "night" through verbal suggestion demonstrates how theatrical skills can reshape reality to serve desire.

The post-coital conversation reveals the fundamental disconnect between their expectations. The Actress's accusation that he treats their intimacy as if "nothing had happened" exposes male aristocratic ability to compartmentalize sexual encounters while maintaining emotional distance.

The Count's postponement of their planned evening meeting until "the day after tomorrow" reveals his need to restore temporal and emotional distance after the unexpected intimacy. His concern for "the soul" provides intellectual justification for what appears to be simple masculine anxiety about entanglement.

For modern readers, "reseda" refers to a plant used in 19th-century perfumery, "courtesy visit" indicates formal social calls with specific time limits and behavioral expectations, and "Steinamanger" was a real Hungarian garrison town that becomes the Actress's dismissive nickname for the Count, reducing him to his provincial military posting.

The Actress's final explosive dismissal ("Farewell, Steinamanger!") transforms her from seductress to dismissive employer, using his military assignment as an insult that strips away his aristocratic pretensions. This reversal of power dynamics demonstrates how theatrical training provides weapons against social hierarchy that can temporarily destabilize traditional class and gender relationships.

CHAPTER 10: "THE COUNT AND THE PROSTITUTE"

THIS FINAL CHAPTER COMPLETES Schnitzler's circular structure by returning to the lowest social stratum, yet featuring the highest-ranking male character in a shabby prostitute's room at dawn. The squalid setting—yellowed blinds, cheap Japanese fans, acrid petroleum lamp—creates stark contrast with the Count's aristocratic status and establishes the moral and physical degradation underlying Vienna's sexual economy.

The Count's disorientation upon waking reflects both alcoholic confusion and psychological displacement, as his aristocratic identity conflicts with his current surroundings. His inability to remember the previous night's events reveals how alcohol enabled class transgression that his conscious mind would normally reject, while his obsessive questioning about what happened betrays deep anxiety about maintaining social boundaries.

Leocadia's matter-of-fact responses to his philosophical questioning demonstrate working-class pragmatism that cuts through aristocratic romanticism. Her statement that she's "in this business for one year" and "going into my twentieth year" reveals both the economic desperation that drove young women into prostitution and the regulated, businesslike nature of Vienna's sex trade.

The Count's unexpected tenderness—examining her sleeping face, commenting on her resemblance to someone from his past—transforms their commercial transaction into something approaching genuine human connection. His observation that "sleep makes one look... like the brother... death" reflects aristocratic literary education while revealing unexpected philosophical depth triggered by her vulnerability.

Leocadia's casual mention of moving to Spiegelgasse with "the madam" and other girls exposes the organized nature of Vienna's prostitution industry, where women lived in managed houses that provided both protection and exploitation. Her description of Milli's schedule—sleeping all day, working all night—illustrates the inverted temporal world of commercial sex work.

The Count's impulse to kiss her eyes "because she reminded me of someone" suggests that aristocratic emotional life involved complex layering of current experiences over past relationships. This romantic gesture in a commercial setting reveals how memory and desire can temporarily transcend class boundaries, though his inability to specify who she resembles indicates repressed or forbidden associations.

Leocadia's reference to Franz the waiter who wants to marry her introduces hope for escape from prostitution through working-class respectability. Her rejection of marriage "not for any price" demonstrates how sex work, despite its dangers, provided economic independence that conventional marriage to a waiter could not match for women with limited options.

The Count's repeated departures and returns reveal psychological conflict between aristocratic duty to maintain class boundaries and genuine attraction to Leocadia's authenticity. His confession that he wants "nothing from you" attempts to distinguish their encounter from purely commercial transactions, though his payment on the nightstand maintains economic hierarchy.

Leocadia's pragmatic observation that "many men who aren't in the mood in the morning" normalizes male sexual dysfunction while revealing her professional experience with aristocratic clients who often visited her after evening drinking. Her unimpressed response to his unusual behavior demonstrates working-class immunity to romantic pretensions.

The Count's final realization that they did have sexual relations the previous night, despite his blackout, restores the encounter to purely physical terms while eliminating any romantic idealization. His acceptance that "it just wasn't meant for me" suggests aristocratic resignation to emotional emptiness despite social privilege.

The chambermaid's correction of his "Good night" to "Good morning" emphasizes temporal disorientation that symbolizes broader social confusion created when class boundaries temporarily dissolve through alcohol and sexual commerce. This minor detail reinforces how aristocratic transgression requires return to normal social order.

For modern readers, "petroleum lamp" refers to kerosene lighting common in poor housing, "on the beat" means working as a street prostitute, and the Count's concern about "wine in my head" reflects aristocratic anxiety about alcohol-induced loss of social control that enabled crossing class boundaries normally maintained through conscious choice.

The circular completion of Schnitzler's work through this encounter between highest and lowest social ranks demonstrates how Vienna's sexual economy ultimately connected all social levels while maintaining rigid hierarchies that prevented genuine equality or lasting human connection across class lines.

APPENDIX

ARTHUR SCHNITZLER BIOGRAPHY

"I write of love and death. □
What other subjects are there?"
- Arthur Schnitzler

ARTHUR SCHNITZLER (15 MAY 1862 – 21 October 1931) was an Austrian author and dramatist. He is considered one of the most significant representatives of the Viennese Modernism. Schnitzler's works, which include psychological dramas and narratives, looked beneath the surface of turn-of-the-century Viennese bourgeois life, making him a sharp and stylistically conscious chronicler of Viennese society around 1900.

Arthur Schnitzler was born in Leopoldstadt, Vienna, the capital of the Austrian Empire. He was the offspring of a distinguished Hungarian doctor, Johann Schnitzler (1835–1893), and Luise Markbreiter (1838–1911), the daughter of the Viennese physician Philipp Markbreiter. Both of his parents hailed from Jewish backgrounds. In 1885, Schnitzler earned a medical doctorate from the University of Vienna. He eventually left the field of medicine to pursue writing.

In 1903, Schnitzler wed Olga Gussmann, a 21-year-old aspiring actress and singer from a Jewish middle-class family. They had a son, Heinrich (1902–1982), on August 9, 1902. In 1909, they had a daughter, Lili, who died by suicide in 1928. The couple separated in 1921. Schnitzler passed away on October 21, 1931, in Vienna, succumbing to a brain hemorrhage.

Schnitzler was a contemporary of Sigmund Freud, who often exchanged letters during their lives. In one such letter, Sigmund Freud admitted, "I have gained the impression that you have learned through intuition – although actually as a result of sensitive introspection – everything that I have had to unearth by laborious work on other persons."

Schnitzler's writings frequently sparked controversy, both for their candid depictions of sexuality and their staunch opposition to anti-semitism, as exemplified by works such as his play *Professor Bernhardi* and his novel *Der Weg ins Freie*. However, despite Schnitzler's Jewish heritage, *Professor Bernhardi* and *Fräulein Else* are among the few of his protagonists who are clearly identified as Jewish.

Schnitzler's play *Reigen*, which featured ten pairs of characters before and after sexual encounters, was labeled as pornographic upon its release, with the criticism couched in virulent anti-Semitic terms. The play was later adapted into a successful French-language film, *La Ronde*, directed by the German-born Max Ophüls in 1950. It gained considerable popularity in the English-speaking world, leading to Schnitzler's work becoming better known under its French title. Additionally, the play has inspired various other film adaptations, including Richard Oswald's *The Merry-Go-Round* (1920), Roger Vadim's *Circle of Love* (1964), Otto Schenk's *Der Reigen* (1973), and a more recent version by Fernando Meirelles.

In the novella *Fräulein Else* (1924), Schnitzler may be countering a controversial criticism of the Jewish character by Otto Weininger (1903) by examining the sexuality of the young female Jewish protagonist. The narrative, told from the first-person perspective of a young aristocratic woman, depicts a moral quandary that culminates in tragedy.

As a member of the avant-garde Young Vienna (Jung-Wien) group, Schnitzler experimented with both formal and social conventions. In his 1900 novella *Leutnant Gustl*, he pioneered the use of stream-of-consciousness narration and internal dialogue in German fiction. The story presents an unflattering depiction of its protagonist and the army's obsessive code of formal honor. This work led to Schnitzler being stripped of his commission as a reserve medical officer, an action that should be understood in the context of the rising tide of antisemitism at the time.

Schnitzler specialized in shorter literary forms like novellas and one-act plays. In his short stories, such as *Die grüne Krawatte* (*The Green Tie*), he demonstrated himself to be a pioneer of microfiction. However, he also wrote two full-length novels: *Der Weg ins Freie*, a brilliant depiction of a segment of pre-World War I Viennese society centered on a talented but unmotivated young composer, and the artistically less successful *Therese*.

In addition to his plays and fiction, Schnitzler meticulously maintained a diary from the age of 17 until two days before his death. The manuscript, spanning nearly 8,000 pages, is most notable for Schnitzler's casual accounts of his sexual exploits; he was often involved with multiple women simultaneously (with a significant number of these liaisons occurring with an embroiderer named "Jeanette") and, for a period, kept a record of every orgasm he experienced. Collections of Schnitzler's letters have also been published.

Schnitzler's literary works were denounced as "Jewish filth" by Adolf Hitler, leading to their prohibition by the Nazis in Austria and Germany. In 1933, amidst Joseph Goebbels' book burnings in Berlin and other urban centers, Schnitzler's writings were fed to the flames alongside those of other Jewish intellectuals, including Einstein, Marx, Kafka, Freud, and Stefan Zweig.

His novella *Fräulein Else* has been adapted several times, including the German silent film *Fräulein Else* (1929), starring Elisabeth Bergner, and the 1946 Argentine film *The Naked Angel*, starring Olga Zubarry.

His novella *Traumnovelle* (*Dream Story*) was adapted into the 1969 German film Traumnovelle, directed by Wolfgang Glück. Most notably,

Stanley Kubrick adapted it into the 1999 film Eyes Wide Shut, starring Tom Cruise and Nicole Kidman. This film version brought Schnitzler's work to a global audience. The film transposed the setting to contemporary New York while remaining remarkably faithful to the themes and atmosphere of the original novella.

Arthur Schnitzler is still celebrated for his innovative use of fragmented narratives and candid examination of sexuality, desire, and the complexities of the human psyche. Schnitzler's legacy is marked by his bold challenges to the moral conventions of his time, paving the way for modernist literature and influencing a generation of writers and dramatists. His profound impact extends beyond literature into theatre and film, as many of his works have been adapted and continue to resonate with contemporary audiences, reflecting ongoing themes of love, betrayal, and existential angst.

SELECTED WORKS BY ARTHUR SCHNITZLER

PLAYS

Anatol (1893)

Flirtation (*Liebelei* – 1895)

Fair Game (*Freiwild* – 1896)

Light-'O-Love (1896)

Reigen (1897)

Die Gefährtin (1899)

Paracelsus (1899)

The Green Cockatoo (*Der grüne Kakadu* – 1899)

The Lonely Way (*Der einsame Weg* – 1904)

Intermezzo (*Zwischenspiel* – 1904)

Der Ruf des Lebens (1906)

Countess Mizzi or the Family Reunion (*Komtesse Mizzi oder Der Familientag* – 1907)

Living Hours (1911)

Young Medardus (*Der junge Medardus* – 1910)

The Vast Domain (*Das weite Land* – 1911)

Professor Bernhardi (1912)

The Comedy of Seduction (*Komödie der Verführung* – 1924)

Comedies of Words and Other Plays (1917)

Novels

The Road into the Open (*Der Weg ins Freie* – 1908)

Therese. Chronik eines Frauenlebens (1928)

Memorial in Vienna

Short stories and novellas

Dying (*Sterben* – 1895)

None but the Brave (*Leutnant Gustl* – 1900)

Berta Garlan (1900)

Blind Geronimo and his Brother (*Der blinde Geronimo und sein Bruder* – 1902)

The Prophecy (*Die Weissagung* – 1905)

Casanova's Homecoming (*Casanovas Heimfahrt* – 1918)

Fräulein Else (1924)

Dream Story (Traumnovelle) (1925/26)

Night Games (*Spiel im Morgengrauen* – 1926)

Flight into Darkness (*Flucht in die Finsternis* – 1931)

The Death of a Bachelor

Late Fame (2014)

Nonfiction

My Youth in Vienna (*Jugend in Wien*), an autobiography published posthumously in 1968

Diary, 1879–1931